Enid Blyton's Enchanted Tales

ADVENTURES IN FAIRYLAND

D1368835

Enid Blyton's
Enchanted Tales

The Magical Shop
Return to the Magical Shop
The Faraway Tree Adventure
The Wizard who Wasn't
Adventures in Fairyland
Magic in Fairyland

Enid Blyton's Enchanted Tales

ADVENTURES IN FAIRYLAND

Illustrated by Gunvor Edwards

RED FOX

A Red Fox Book

Published by Random House Children's Books
20 Vauxhall Bridge Road, London SW1V 2SA

A division of The Random House Group Ltd
London Melbourne Sydney Auckland
Johannesburg and agencies throughout the world

1 3 5 7 9 10 8 6 4 2

These stories first appeared in Enid Blyton's Sunny Stories magazine.
First published in book form as Tales From Fairyland by Red Fox 1993.

Red Fox edition 2000

Printed and bound in Great Britain by
Cox and Wyman Ltd, Reading, Berkshire

THE RANDOM HOUSE GROUP Limited Reg. No. 954009

www.randomhouse.co.uk

ISBN 0 09 940806 6

Contents

Contents

The Sulkabit Wizard

Once upon a time there lived a wizard called Sulkabit. He really ought to have been called Sulka*lot*, because he was for ever frowning and growling and sulking.

He lived in the village of Merryheart. It wasn't a very big village, but everybody was merry there, for it was the prettiest, sunniest little spot in the whole of Fairyland.

The happiest person there was plump Mother Runaround. She lived all alone in Laughing Cottage at the end of the village. Everybody liked her because she was always running around doing all sorts of odd jobs for this person and that, and she always had a large smile ready for anybody she met.

No, I shouldn't have said *every*body liked her because one person didn't, and that was the Sulkabit Wizard. He couldn't bear her because she laughed at him.

He was always shaking his head and saying something terrible was going to happen, and Mother Runaround would never believe him.

'I'm sure there will be an earthquake tomorrow,' he said. 'If not here, then somewhere else. It would be more fitting for you to sigh than to laugh, Mother Runaround.'

'Bless my button boots!' cried Mother Runaround, setting her basket down. 'What happened to the great black storm you said was going to come last week? And what about the plague of caterpillars you told me of? *I* never saw anything of them.'

'They happened somewhere,' said the Sulk-

abit Wizard, crossly, 'and they might have happened here, for all *you* were to know!'

'I'll wait till they come, then, before I begin to worry!' laughed Mother Runaround. 'You're a funny sort of person to live in the Village of Merryheart, Sulkabit! You ought to go and live in Doleful Town, where everyone sighs and groans, instead of laughs!'

And with that, Mother Runaround picked up her basket and went off to give a pot of her new honey to Hoppetty Ho, who lived at the top of the hill.

Sulkabit looked after her. He saw a tribe of little pixies dance up to her and take her basket from her to carry. He saw Fairy Tiptoes fly up and kiss her. He saw Toddles, the baby of the village, run up and give her a bunch of flowers out of his very own garden.

'*I* don't know why they all like her so much,' he grumbled. 'Nobody ever carries *my* basket for me, or gives *me* anything!'

Pinkity Pixie came trotting by him just then, and the Sulkabit Wizard called out to him.

'Hey, Pinkity! Come and carry my basket for me. Why don't you help me as you help Mother Runaround?'

'Ho, help the Sulkabit Wizard!' laughed Pinkity. 'Not I! Your frowns and groans are enough to chase anyone away, and we all know that some of your magic is bad magic! *We* don't want to be turned into beetles and toads!'

He ran away, laughing, and Sulkabit was left standing alone, looking as cross as two sticks.

It was quite true that some of his magic was bad magic. When he had been cross with the Knobbly Gnome, he had put a bad spell in the Gnome's front garden, and all his cabbages grew prickles, so that the Knobbly Gnome couldn't pick them, and was as frightened as could be.

And another time he had done a bad turn to the Bee-Woman, and made all her honey turn pink, so that she was afraid to eat it.

The Sulkabit Wizard went home, muttering and grumbling, wishing he could do Mother Runaround a bad turn too.

'I must be careful, though,' he said to himself, 'for if any one guesses I have done it, I shall be turned out of Merryheart Village, there's no doubt of that.'

So he sat down and he thought and thought what he could do, and at last he thought of a plan.

'Ho, ho!' he chuckled, 'ho, ho! I'll make a

cake and I'll put a spell in it. Then I'll take the cake to Mother Runaround and give it to her. When she eats it the spell will work, and no-one will know anything about how she got it!'

What do you think the spell was? It was that anyone who ate the cake should at once begin to give away every single thing in the house, and only stop when there was nothing left at all!

'Ho, ho!' chuckled the Wizard again. 'I'd like to see old Mother Runaround's face when she sees herself giving away her chairs and her tables, her pictures and her kettles! She *will* feel funny when she stands in the middle of her empty cottage. What fun it will be!'

He at once set to work to make the cake. It was quite an ordinary cake to look at, yellow inside and brown on top. Sulkabit baked it well, popped the spell inside, let it cool, and then wrapped it up in a newspaper.

'Perhaps I'd better not let Mother Runaround know it's from me,' he decided. 'She might think it rather funny.'

So he wrote a message on a card, and slipped it in the parcel. It just said 'From a friend' and nothing more.

That night, when it was dark, and everyone

in Merryheart was asleep, the Sulkabit Wizard
crept out of his cottage and went to Mother
Runaround's. He put the parcel on her doorstep and then crept back to his cottage again.

'Now we shall see something funny soon!'
he said, rubbing his hands together. 'Old
Mother Runaround won't be laughing very
much for a few weeks, and she will be very
sorry she ever laughed at me!'

Now next morning, when Mother Runaround opened her door, she found the parcel.

'Dear me, whatever can this be?' she said,
and took it indoors. She unpacked it, and
found the cake with the message that said
'From a friend.'

'From a friend!' she said. 'Now whoever can that be, I wonder!'

She couldn't think who it could be, and she popped the cake into the larder for tea-time. But it hadn't been there very long when Mother Runaround remembered she had bought a fine new cake the day before.

'It does seem greedy to have two cakes in the house!' she said. 'I really think I must give one away to somebody. I'd better give the one I found on the doorstep, because I've cut a piece out of the other one.'

So she took it out of the larder, and set it on the table. She fetched a nice piece of white paper and wrapped it round the cake. Then she tied it with a bright piece of blue ribbon, for Mother Runaround didn't believe in wrapping a cake up in newspaper and dirty old string.

Then she set off to go to the Knobbly Gnome's at the other end of the village. When she got there she found he was out, so she left the cake on his kitchen table with a note to say that it was for him.

'I don't expect he gets many cakes,' she said to herself as she went home, 'so I think he'll be very pleased.'

13

When the Knobbly Gnome got home, he undid the parcel and found the cake.

'Dear, dear!' he said, 'a fine new cake from Mother Runaround, and I'm going away tomorrow so I can't eat it! What a pity! Never mind, I'll give it to someone else. I know she won't mind.'

He wrapped it up again, and wondered whom to take it to.

'I'll give it to the Fiddle-de-dee Elf!' he decided. 'She is not very well, so she will be pleased to have a nice present.'

He popped it into a basket and ran off. The Fiddle-de-dee Elf's servant came to the door when he got there and took the parcel from the Knobbly Gnome.

She ran to give it to the Elf, who was in bed, feeling rather weak.

'A present!' cried the little servant.

The Fiddle-de-dee Elf untied the blue ribbon and unwrapped the cake.

'Oh!' she cried, 'it's a lovely cake – but oh dear me, the doctor says I'm not to eat cake for a whole week! How very, very disappointing!'

'Give it to Greeneyes the Goblin,' said the little servant. 'It's his birthday today!'

'Wrap it up again and take it to him, then,' said the Elf. 'He will love it.'

The servant wrapped it up again neatly, put on her hat, and ran off. Greeneyes lived quite near, so it wasn't very long before she had knocked at the door and delivered the parcel.

Greeneyes wondered what it could be. He opened it, and groaned when he saw the cake.

'That's the fifth cake I've had given me for my birthday!' he said. 'Whatever shall I do with it? I really can't eat five. I must give it away to someone else.'

He tied it up again and wondered whom to take it to.

'I'll give it to Frisky the Squirrel,' he decided. 'He's a dear little fellow, and I'm sure he'll like it.'

So off he went with the cake.

But Frisky had gone to sleep for the winter and didn't want to wake up again yet.

'Cake!' he said sleepily. 'Don't want cake now, Greeneyes. Give it to the Skippitty Pixie, who lives in the next tree to mine.'

Greeneyes went to the next tree, and found Skippitty was not there.

He saw a note stuck up on the tree. It said: –

```
·GONE OUT.
BACK SOON.
```

'Oh well, I'll pop the cake inside his door,' thought Greeneyes, 'and he'll find it when he comes back.'

So he put the cake down and went home again.

Very soon Skippitty came home, and nearly fell over the cake inside his door.

'What in the world is this?' he cried, and picked it up. He put it on his little table and unwrapped it.

'A cake!' he cried. 'And oh dear, I hate cake! What a pity it wasn't biscuits! Whatever shall I do with it?'

He sat down and thought.

'I'll go and give it to the Sulkabit Wizard!'

he said at last. 'Nobody ever has a kind word for him, and maybe this will make him glad.'

So he carefully wrapped the cake up again in its nice white paper, and tied the blue ribbon round it. Then he put on his little pointed cap and set off for the Wizard's cottage.

When he got there he knocked loudly. The Wizard came to the door.

'I've brought a present for you,' said Skippitty, rather nervously. 'I hope you will like it.'

The Sulkabit Wizard took the parcel, muttered a grumpy thank you, and shut the door.

He put the parcel down on the table. He was really rather excited about it, for he hadn't had a present for a very long time.

'I hope it's something to eat,' he said, 'because I really feel rather hungry, and there's only dry bread in the cupboard!'

He opened the parcel and found the cake. He didn't guess for one moment that it was the very same cake he had made the day before. He thought that that cake was safely at Mother Runaround's, waiting to be eaten.

'A cake!' he cried. 'Just what I wanted! I'll make a good meal of it.'

He fetched a knife, cut the cake, and ate a

large slice. It was good, so he ate another. Then he ate a third.

'I may as well eat the lot,' he said. 'It's not a very big cake.'

So he ate it all. Little did he know that a powerful spell was mixed in with it!

Soon the spell began to work. The Wizard looked around his room.

'I think I'll take that nice cosy little chair of mine and give it to Mother Runaround,' he found himself saying.

Then, to his own great surprise, his legs walked over to the chair, his hands picked it up, and off he went to Laughing Cottage. He didn't really want to go one bit, but he couldn't help it.

When he got there his tongue said: —

'This is for you, Mother Runaround, with my love,' and his hands pushed the chair into Mother Runaround's cottage.

Mother Runaround was tremendously astonished. She took the chair, and stared at Sulkabit.

'Perhaps he's sorry he's so sulky and cross,' she thought to herself. 'Perhaps he's trying to make up for it. I must be nice to him.'

So she smiled kindly at him, and thanked him in her nicest voice.

Sulkabit went back to his cottage, and took up a table. He went with it to Hoppetty Ho's, all the way up the hill, and gave it to him. He didn't want to, but he really couldn't help it. He was most astonished at himself, and he couldn't think what had happened to him.

He gave away all his chairs, his bed, his carpet, his pictures, his kettles and his crockery. He gave his books to Greeneyes and his clock to Fiddle-de-dee.

Everybody was surprised at him, for all in Merryheart Village knew him to be a cross and surly old wizard. Still, everyone thought he was trying his best to be kind and generous, and they smiled at him and thanked him very

prettily. Some of them kissed him, and Sulka-bit was surprised to find he liked it.

'It's really very nice to be smiled at and kissed,' he thought. 'No wonder Mother Run-around always laughs and looks happy, for everyone smiles at her and loves her. But what-ever can be the matter with me? I seem to be under a magic spell.'

Not until Sulkabit's cottage was quite empty, and he stood lonely and puzzled in the middle of his bare floor, did he guess what had happened to him.

'I've eaten my own cake!' he suddenly groaned. 'Yes, that's what I've done! That cake must have been the one I made, but someone had wrapped it up in white paper and tied it with blue ribbon and I didn't think it was the same one. Oh dear, oh dear, I am punished indeed for my bad thoughts. Still, I have had more smiles and kisses today than Mother Runaround, I'm sure, and my heart is warm tonight, even if my hands are not.'

He shivered. Then he went out to the barn and took a great armful of hay. He made himself a bed on the bare floor, and went to sleep.

When Pop-in the postman called next morning, he was astonished to see Sulkabit lying asleep on the floor, with all his furniture gone. He called everyone to see, and soon all the village knew that Sulkabit had given away everything he had, and had nothing left for himself.

'We made a mistake about him,' they said in surprise. 'He is good and generous after all. Let's wake him and tell him we want to be friends with him.'

So for the first time in his life Sulkabit was awakened by kisses and kind names, and he could hardly believe his eyes and ears when he sat up and saw smiling, kindly faces all around him.

'We want to be friends with you, dear old Sulkabit,' said the little people.

Sulkabit remembered how he had been caught by his own spell – but he made up his mind never to tell anyone about it.

'I will be kind because I want to, now, not because of a spell,' he said to himself, and he smiled at everyone around him.

And from that very day he changed, and nobody ever knew why. Only *I* knew, and now I have told all the secret to you!

The Clockwork Bear

There was once a clockwork bear who could walk on all his four brown legs when he was wound up. He was a nice little fellow with a brown fur coat, little eyes and a stumpy tail. He lived in the toy cupboard with all the other toys and they were very fond of him.

He belonged to Janie and Dick. They loved to play with him and make him walk right across the nursery floor. One day they took him out into the garden to play.

They had a tea-party, and the bear, the clown, the bunny-in-the-green-coat and the big doll all came to the party and sat or stood around. It was great fun.

Then Dick wound up the clockwork bear and set him walking across the lawn – and at

that very moment Mummy put her head out of the window and called them.

'Janie! Dick!' she cried. 'Here's Uncle Jim to see you!'

Both the children rushed indoors at once, for they loved Uncle Jim. The toys were quite forgotten. The clockwork bear walked steadily on over the grass, and nobody noticed him.

When Nurse came to pick up the toys and bring them in she didn't look for the bear, for she had forgotten about him. She went indoors with the bunny-in-the-green-coat, the big doll and the clown.

The clockwork bear went on walking. He came to the edge of the grass and walked down the path. He walked over a flower-bed and came to another path. He walked down that and came to the garden gate. It led out into the lane at the back and, as it was wide open, the bear walked out. He didn't want to go out at all, but, you see, he was wound up and he couldn't stop walking even if he wanted to. So out into the lane he went.

He walked into the ditch at the side, and suddenly a very angry voice cried out in his ear:

'Look where you're going! You nearly walked over my nest!'

The bear looked round. It was a robin calling to him and the bear saw that he had almost walked over her pretty nest, in which lay four spotted eggs.

'Sorry,' said the bear. 'I couldn't help it!'

Then another voice cried out crossly and the bear jumped in alarm. This time it was the hedgehog.

'Didn't you see me hurrying along the bottom of the ditch?' cried the hedgehog. 'You almost stood on me!'

'Sorry!' said the clockwork bear, walking on. 'I couldn't help it!'

'Well, you might at least stop walking!' shouted the angry hedgehog.

But the bear *couldn't* stop! On he went through the ditch, walking, walking, walking!

Soon he saw a spider's web right in front of him. It was a beautiful web, just finished that morning. It hung between two green nettles, swaying gently in the breeze.

The bear saw it – but, of course, he couldn't stop walking! He went straight at the web.

The spider that hung in the middle of it ran quickly up the web and hid under a nettle leaf. Then it called out angrily to the bear:

'Hi! Look where you're going! There's my web in front of you! If you walk into it you'll break it, and it's only just finished this afternoon!'

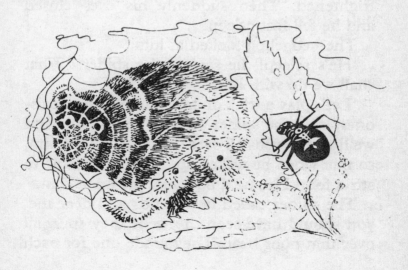

Well, the bear couldn't stop himself. He just walked straight into it and broke it all to rags! The spider was so angry that it began to shout rudely after the bear. The hedgehog and the robin came up and they shouted, too.

'Sorry!' called the clockwork bear. 'I couldn't help it!'

The spider, the hedgehog and the robin all ran after the bear. Suddenly the clockwork ran down and the bear stopped. He couldn't walk any more. The robin pecked him hard. The hedgehog pricked him with his prickles and the spider tried to bite him. The clockwork bear felt most unhappy.

He stood there in the ditch, very tired and frightened. Then suddenly his eyes closed and he fell fast asleep!

The hedgehog looked at him.

'He's asleep!' he said to the spider. 'What shall we do with him?'

'Let's play a trick on him and take him prisoner,' said the spider. 'I'll get my friends and we'll weave webs all over him and around him, so that when he wakes up he won't be able to stir a foot! Ho, he'll be a real prisoner!'

The spider called her friends and dear me, you should have seen the webs they spun all over that poor bear. They made one for each foot, fastening it to the ground with silken threads. They fastened his tail to his body so that he wouldn't be able to move it. They spun webs all over him, even across his nose!

The web on his nose made him sneeze – a-tishoo! That woke him up. My goodness me, how frightened he was to find that the spiders had spun webs all over him!

'Ho ho!' laughed the spiders, the robin and the hedgehog. 'Now you're punished! You can't move a foot!'

Well, of course, the clockwork was run down, so the bear couldn't walk a step, even if he tried. The creatures around him didn't know that – they really thought that the webs had made him prisoner and they were full of glee at their cleverness.

Goodness knows what would have happened to the poor clockwork bear if the other toys hadn't remembered him and come looking for him that night. The clown, the bunny-in-the-green-coat, and the big doll found him standing there in the ditch, crying big tears out of his little brown eyes.

'Oh, you poor thing!' cried the toys, running to him. 'We've come to save you.'

'He's a prisoner,' said the hedgehog. 'The

spiders have fastened him to the ground. He can't move a step.'

'That's all *you* know!' said the clown, rudely. 'You've no business to take a bear prisoner.'

'Well, he didn't look where he was going,' said the robin, crossly. 'He nearly walked over my nest, he almost trod on the hedgehog, and he broke the spider's new web.'

'He didn't mean to,' said the toys. 'He's a very kind little fellow. He just couldn't help it. The spider can easily make another web.'

'Well, we've punished the bear,' said the spider, boastfully. 'Look! He can't move! He's been standing there for ages, and he can't move a step!'

The boys laughed.

'He'll soon break all the webs around him!' they said. 'You just watch!'

The clown wound up the clockwork bear. Then the toys all climbed up on his back. He lifted his feet and began to walk! You should have seen how he broke all the thin spider-threads! They snapped in two at once!

'Here I go, out of your webs!' called the bear. 'I'm sorry I offended you, but I couldn't help it. I told you I was sorry!'

The toys guided him out of the ditch and he walked back up the lane, through the open

gate, and into the garden. The nursery was upstairs and as the bear couldn't climb stairs, the toys took him to the summer-house and there they stayed with him all night long.

Janie and Dick found them there in the morning and they couldn't *think* how they came to be there.

'I can tell you!' trilled the robin, nearby. 'I can tell you!'

And he sang a song all about how the bear had been taken prisoner and had escaped. The children listened, but they couldn't understand.

'Isn't that robin singing beautifully?' they

said. 'It seems as if he wants to tell us something!'

Off flew the robin to talk to the hedgehog. As for the spider, she made another web far better than the first, and very soon forgot all about the clockwork bear.

The Goblin Looking Glass

It was a very wet day, and Micky and Pam couldn't go out to play in the garden. They were cross about it because they wanted to dig in their sandpit. They stood at the window and grumbled.

'It's no use being cross, my dears,' said Nurse. 'Get your bricks or your books and amuse yourselves. I am going down to help Mummy make a new dress for Pam, so be good whilst I am gone.'

Nurse took her work-basket and went downstairs. The children were left alone. They turned away from the window and stared around the nursery.

'I don't want to play with bricks,' said Micky. 'And I'm tired of all my books. I wish something exciting would happen.'

'Nothing lovely *ever* happens!' sighed Pam. 'You read of such glorious adventures in books – but nothing ever *really* happens to children like us.'

'There isn't even anything very exciting in the nursery,' said Micky. 'We haven't a gramophone like Peter Brown has. And we haven't a nice clockwork railway like Jack's. There's nothing nice in our nursery at all.'

'No, nothing – except that big looking-glass,' said Pam, pointing to a full-length mirror hung on the wall. The children liked this very much because they could see all of themselves in it, from top to toe. Around the mirror was carved a most exciting pattern of fruits, flowers and tiny little goblin-like creatures peeping out from the flowers. It really was a lovely looking-glass.

Pam and Micky liked to look into it and see their nursery reflected there, the other way round. Micky looked at the mirror on that wet, rainy morning, and an idea came into his head.

'I wonder if there is anything magic about that mirror,' he said, going over to it. 'You know, it's very, very old, Pam. Let's look carefully at all those little goblins carved around it and see if we think there's any magic about them.'

So the two children looked carefully at each goblin, and rubbed each one to see if anything happened. But nothing did. Micky was disappointed. He leaned against the mirror and looked into it at the nursery reflected there.

And then he saw a most strange and curious thing. He saw standing in the mirror-nursery a little, carved chair, just by the fire-place – but when he looked back into the real nursery there was no chair at all!

'Pam! Pam! Look here!' he cried, excitedly. 'Look into the mirror. Do you see that funny carved chair standing by the fire-place? Well, it's in the mirror, but it isn't in our nursery! What do you think of that!'

Pam looked. Sure enough, it was just as Micky had said. A small carved chair stood in the looking-glass – but it wasn't in the real nursery at all. It was only in the looking-glass. It was carved like the mirror itself, and seemed to match it perfectly. Whose was it? Who sat there? And why was it in the looking-glass but not in the nursery itself?

'Pam, Pam! Something exciting has happened at last!' cried Micky. He pressed his face against the glass to try and see further

into the mirror – and suddenly he gave a great cry of surprise and fell right through the mirror into the reflection beyond!

Pam stared in astonishment. There was Micky on the other side of the mirror, staring at her, too surprised to speak. Then she heard his voice, sounding rather far away.

'Pam! I'm the other side of the mirror! Take my hand and come too. We'll have a real adventure!'

Pam stretched out her hand and took Micky's. He gave her a pull and she passed right through the looking-glass and stood beside Micky. They looked back at their nursery – and as they looked, they saw the door open and Nurse come in.

'Don't let her see us,' whispered Micky. 'It would spoil everything. Quick, hide!'

He ran out of the door in the mirror with Pam. They expected to find themselves on the broad, sunny landing that lay outside their own nursery door – but the looking-glass house was different. Instead of a wide landing there was a narrow, dark passage. Micky stopped.

'This is funny,' he said. 'It's quite different from our house. I wonder where we really are, now.'

Pam felt a bit frightened and wanted to go back, but Micky wouldn't let her. No, this was an adventure, and he wanted to go on with it.

'There's nothing to be afraid of,' he said. 'I'll look after you.'

He took Pam along the dark passage and came at last to stairs going up and down. They were peculiar stairs, going in a spiral, and the children wondered whether to go up them or down them. They decided to go up them.

So up they went and came at last to a big, grey door set with orange nails. They pushed it open and looked inside. And they saw a very strange sight!

A small goblin-like man, with funny, pointy ears, sat hunched up in a corner by a big fireplace, leaning over a large red book. Tears were running down his cheeks and made a big pool at his feet. The children stared at him in surprise.

'What's the matter?' asked Micky, at last. The goblin jumped so much with fright that his book nearly fell into the fire. He snatched it out and sat down again on his stool, holding his hand to his beating heart.

'Oh!' he said. 'Oh! What a fright you gave me! I thought you were Bom, the big goblin. How in the world did you get here?'

'Oh, never mind that,' said Micky. 'We *are* here that's all. What were you crying for?'

'Look at this book,' said the goblin, beginning to cry again. 'It's a book of recipes. I've got to make some special lemonade for Bom, and I can't read very well, so I just simply can't find out how to make it! There are such long words here – and Bom will whip me and stand me in a corner all night if I haven't got the lemonade ready when he comes back.'

'*I'll* read it for you!' said Micky. He took the book and read out loud.

'Enchanted Lemonade. To Make – Take the juice of five lemons that have grown best in

36

moonlight. Take some yellow honey from the bumble-bee that visits the night-shade on Friday evening. Take a spoonful of blue sugar. Stir with a kingfisher's feather. Say five enchanted words over the mixture.'

'Oh, thank you!' cried the small goblin, delighted. 'Now I know exactly what to do. Oh, you really are kind and clever. I'll make the lemonade at once!'

He took five strange-looking, silvery lemons from a dish in a cupboard. Then he found a tiny flute in one of his pockets and blew on it. In a moment or two a very large bumble-bee flew in at the open window. The goblin spoke to it in a curious humming voice, and the bee flew out. It came back in a few minutes with a small jar of yellow honey, which the goblin took from it with a smile. Then out flew the bee again.

Micky and Pam watched in amazement. The goblin shook some blue sugar from a bag into a silver spoon and mixed it with the juice of the lemons and the honey. Then he took a bright blue feather from a jar and stirred the mixture, muttering over it the strangest words that the children had ever heard.

'There! It's made!' said the goblin, happily, putting the bowl of lemonade on the window-sill. 'Thanks to you, little boy! But, tell me – what are you doing here in Bom's house? Does he know you are here?'

'No,' said Micky. 'I didn't even know it was Bom's house. We came through the mirror in our nursery, and found everything quite different.'

'You came through the mirror!' cried the little goblin, in fright. 'Oh, be careful, then! It's years and years since anyone did that. It's a sort of trap, you know. Bom always hopes someone will fall through that magic mirror one day, and then he finds them and makes them his servants for a hundred years. They are allowed to go back then, but, of course, they are old and so they never want to. They always end up as goblins, like me.'

Micky and Pam listened in astonishment and dismay. They wanted an adventure, but not a horrid one.

'Where is Bom?' asked Micky. 'Perhaps we can get back to our nursery before he sees us.'

'I don't think you can,' said the goblin. 'I believe I can hear him coming now. Quick, take these – they may help you sometime or other. Go and hide behind that couch. Maybe Bom won't see you then.'

Micky took what the goblin pressed into his

hand and then dragged Pam behind the couch. It was only just in time. The door opened and through it came a magnificent goblin, dressed in a cloak of pure gold and a tunic of silver with sapphire buttons. His hat, which he hadn't bothered to take off, had a wonderful curling feather in it, and his long, pointed ears stuck out below it.

'Ho, Tumpy!' said Bom, in a loud voice. 'Have you made that lemonade? Where is it?'

Tumpy, the little goblin, ran to the window-sill and fetched the bowl of lemonade. To the children's surprise Bom raised it to his lips and drank it all off at one gulp.

'That's good,' he said. 'Very good.'

Then he stood and sniffed the air as if he could smell something.

'Tumpy,' he said, in an angry voice. 'You have had visitors. Where are they?'

Tumpy was very frightened but he wasn't going to give the children away. He shook his head and, taking up a broom, began to sweep the floor. But Bom took him up in his big hand and shook him so hard that Micky and Pam were sure they could hear his teeth rattling together.

Micky was not going to let anyone be hurt

for him. So he stepped boldly out from behind the couch with Pam.

'Stop shaking Tumpy,' he said. 'We are not really his visitors. We didn't come to see him.'

Bom dropped Tumpy in surprise, and stared at the two children.

'Did you come to see *me*, then?' he asked. 'Oh, perhaps you are the two children of the Wizard Broody? He told me he was sending them out travelling, and that they might perhaps call and see me.'

'Perhaps we are, and perhaps we aren't,' said Micky, grandly. 'We shall not tell you our names.'

Bom looked at them sharply.

'Well, if you are, you can do two or three things for me,' he said. 'I've a silver canary that won't sing. If you are the Wizard's children, you can easily make it sing for me. Then I've a sack of stones I can't turn into gold, no matter how I try. You can do that for me, too. Then I've a candle that won't light. You must make it light for me. If you can do those things I shall know you are the wizard's children and you shall go in safety. But – if you cannot do them, then who will you be? Perhaps children that have come through the goblin mirror! Aha!'

Micky put a bold face on, and hoped that Pam would try not to cry. He meant to go back to the mirror-room as soon as he had a chance, and climb through the looking-glass into his own nursery.

'I'll try to do what you want,' he said. 'Take us to the canary.'

Bom marched to the door, and the children went after him. Micky looked behind him at the little goblin Tumpy, and saw that he was pointing and signalling to him. Micky knew why. It was to remind him that Tumpy had given him something. He patted his pocket to show Tumpy he remembered, and then followed the big goblin down the curly stairs.

41

Bom took them to a little room. There was only one thing in it and that was a big golden cage with a silver canary in it. The little bird sat glumly on its perch, and its bright eyes looked at Bom and the children when they came in.

'This is the canary,' said Bom. 'He won't sing. Let me see you make him open his mouth and trill sweetly.'

'Oh, no, we cannot let you see our magic,' said Micky, much to Pam's surprise. 'You must leave us alone, and come back in half-an-hour. We cannot do magic with a goblin looking on.'

'Very well,' said Bom, and he left the room. Micky was delighted. He waited until the goblin was gone and then he ran to the door.

'We can easily escape before he comes back,' he whispered to Pam. But alas! The door was locked on the outside. The children were prisoners.

Pam began to cry, but Micky wasted no time. He felt in his pocket to see what the little goblin Tumpy had given him. He took the things out. There was a blue feather, very tiny. A shining golden button – and a very small key. That was all.

'Well, I don't know what use these are going

to be,' said Micky, dolefully. 'A feather, a button and a key!'

'Sh!' said Pam, suddenly. 'Can you hear something?'

Micky stood still and listened. He heard a whispering coming through the keyhole of the locked door. It must be Tumpy!

'Stroke the canary with the blue feather!' said the whispering voice. 'Stroke the canary with the blue feather!'

Micky at once took the feather and stuck it between the bars of the golden cage. He began to stroke the canary with the blue feather. He did it until he was quite tired, and then he asked Pam to take a turn too. So she stroked

the canary for a long time. But he didn't make a movement, and he didn't sing a note. It was disappointing.

'That horrid big goblin will be back again soon,' sighed Micky, still stroking the canary. 'Oh, I wonder if this is any use.'

Just as he said that, the canary gave a tiny chirruping noise. Then it suddenly took the blue feather in its beak and tucked it into the silvery feathers that grew from its throat. Micky watched in surprise.

The canary hopped up and down in its cage. Then it opened its mouth and began to sing. How it sang! It was the loudest song the children had ever heard! The door burst open and in came Bom, looking very surprised and pleased.

'Well, well, I didn't think you'd do that so quickly!' he cried. 'The Wizard Broody must have taught you a great deal of magic! Now come to change my sack of stones into gold for me! Ho ho! You shall have a great feast and two big precious stones for yourselves when your tasks are finished!'

The children left the singing canary and once more followed Bom, this time into a curious little room hung round with black curtains, embroidered with goldfish. In the middle was a big sack. Bom pulled it open at the neck. It was full of stones.

'Here you are,' he said. 'Change these into gold for me. I'll go away again if you don't like me to watch you.'

He went out and banged the door. Once more Micky ran to it and tried it – but no, it was fast locked. He stared in despair at the sack. Then he looked behind all the curtains to see if there was a door or window there but there wasn't. The only light came from a great lantern hung from the low ceiling.

'Micky! There's that whispering again!' said Pam, in a low voice. Micky rushed to the door and listened. Once more a tiny whisper came through the keyhole. 'Put the shiny button in the sack. Put the shiny button in the sack.'

'It must be Tumpy again,' said Micky, gladly. 'What a good thing we were able to help him make that magic lemonade, Pam!'

He took the golden button from his pocket and slipped it in the sack. It fell down between the stones and disappeared. Micky watched to see what would happen, quite expecting the stones to turn at once to gold. But they didn't.

The children watched and watched them – but they still remained grey stones. They were afraid Bom would come back – and goodness me, just as they were thinking he surely must be back soon, they heard the door opening. It was Bom!

Micky shut the sack quickly, hoping that he and Pam could slip out of the door before Bom could see the stones had not changed to gold. But the wily Bom had locked the door behind him!

He pulled open the sack – and to the children's great amazement they saw that the stones had changed to shining gold after all! There they were, yellow and bright. They must have changed just as the goblin came into the room.

'Smart children!' said Bom, pleased. 'Clever children! I didn't think you'd be able to do that! I shall write and tell your father you are very clever indeed. Now come and light the candle that won't light! Then you shall have a grand feast, and go home with two fine emeralds in your pockets!'

Micky and Pam followed him to yet another room, this time set with many sunny windows. On a blue table was a tall golden candlestick and in it stood a blue candle.

'This is a witch's candle,' said Bom. 'If only I could light it, it would burn for ever. Light it for me. I will leave you alone for a while.'

Out he went and locked the door behind him. Micky ran to listen to any whispering that might come – but oh dear me, Bom must have come back and caught poor Tumpy at the key-hole, for hardly had the whispering begun than there came the sound of an angry voice, and several sharp slaps. Then somebody began to cry and was hustled away.

'That was poor old Tumpy, I expect,' said Micky. 'Now we shan't know how to light that witch-candle! Well, I've only got one thing left, and that's a little key. I'll see if I can do anything with that.'

He took it out and ran it up and down the candle. Then he struck a match from a box lying nearby and tried to light the candle. But no, it wouldn't light. Micky did everything he could think of, but it wasn't a bit of good. Nothing would make that strange blue candle light.

Pam was looking out of one of the windows. Not one of them would open, but she was looking out to see what lay beyond. There was a wonderful garden set with big, brilliant flowers, and flying about were the brightest, strangest birds she had ever seen. Pam stared as if she couldn't believe her eyes. Then she saw something else.

'Micky!' she called. 'Come here! Look at these two strange children coming up the path to the house.'

Micky looked. Certainly the children were strange. They both had on pointed hats, and long, sweeping cloaks on which were embroidered moons, suns and stars. They carried long, golden sticks in their hands.

'Goodness!' cried Micky, suddenly. 'They must be the Wizard's children – the ones he mistook *us* for! *Now* what are we going to do? Bom will soon know we are not the right children, and he will be very angry! Oh dear, whatever shall we do?'

Pam looked wildly around the room – and suddenly her eyes caught sight of a very small door, not more than eighteen inches high, set at the foot of one of the walls.

'Look, Micky!' she cried. 'There's a tiny door over there! Do you think we might perhaps open it and squeeze through?'

Micky looked – and in a moment he was down on his knees trying to open it. But it was locked! He groaned.

'Try that tiny key you've got!' whispered Pam, in excitement. 'It might fit!'

Micky tried it, with trembling hands. It fitted! He turned it in the lock and pushed

open the door. And at that very moment there came an angry voice outside the room, and the children heard the big door opening.

'I'll punish them!' cried Bom's voice. 'Telling me they were Wizard children when they weren't! I'll make them my servants for a hundred years! Ho ho!'

Micky pushed Pam through the tiny door and then squeezed hurriedly through himself, just as Bom rushed into the room. The angry goblin saw them going through the little door and he rushed over to them. But he was far too big to get through himself!

'I'll go around the other way and catch you!' he roared.

The children found themselves in a low passage. They stumbled along – and suddenly

Micky felt a little hand in his, and a voice spoke to him.

'Don't be afraid, it's only me, Tumpy! I've come to guide you to the looking-glass room. If we're quick we shall get there before Bom does.'

Micky was so glad to have Tumpy! He hurried along with him, Pam following close behind. Down long, twisty passages they went, in and out of funny little rooms, upstairs and downstairs and once through a dim, dark cellar. It was terribly exciting.

At last Tumpy pushed them into a room that seemed very familiar. Yes, it was the looking-glass room at last! It was just like their nursery. Over on the wall was the long mirror.

'Quick! Quick! He's coming!' cried Tumpy, and the two children heard the sound of hurried footsteps and a loud, angry voice.

Micky rushed to the mirror and leapt through it. He helped Pam through too, and then suddenly thought of dragging the little goblin Tumpy through too. It seemed such a shame to leave him behind to the cross and unkind Bom. So he went through too!

Micky looked around. He was in his own, proper nursery. How glad he was! So was Pam. Micky looked into the glass. He saw Bom the big goblin suddenly appear there, shaking his fist at them. Then he faded away, and Micky could see nothing but the reflection of his own nursery. Not even the funny little goblin chair was there now.

Tumpy heard footsteps outside the nursery door and he jumped out of the window. 'I'll come back again tonight!' he whispered.

Nurse came into the room, smiling.

'Well, have you been good children?' she asked.

'Oh yes,' said Micky. 'We've had a lovely time!'

'That's splendid,' said Nurse. 'Well, it's stopped raining, so you can go out. Go and get your rubber boots.'

They went, and when they were in the dark hall-cupboard, putting on their boots, Micky spoke to Pam in a low voice.

'Did it all really happen, Pam? Or did we imagine it? *Did* we go through that looking-glass?'

'Yes, rather!' said Pam. 'Anyway, Tumpy came back with us. You can ask *him* if it was true or not, when he comes to see us tonight! What an adventure we've had!'

And now they are waiting to see Tumpy again. I *wish* I could see him too!

In UpandDown Land

Tom was a very lucky boy, because he had boxes and boxes of meccano. Have you any meccano sets? If you have, you will know what fine things you can make with it! Tom was very clever. He could make bridges, cranes, motors, engines – all kinds of things. He made things up out of his head, and all his friends used to come and admire them. There stood the wonderful things he made, in the middle of the nursery, shining and grand! Even his father used to come and see them, and sometimes he helped Tom.

Now Tom had no time for books, and he didn't even like to be told stories, though he sometimes listened to the Children's Hour. But whenever he heard a fairy story beginning he used to switch off the wireless at once.

'Pooh! Fairies!' he would say. 'There aren't

any! Why don't they tell stories about how to make viaducts and dams and wonderful things like that? When I grow up I'm going to be an engineer!'

Tom often wished he had a big garden with a stream running through it, so that he might make bridges and dams, and all kinds of interesting, *real* things – but all he had was a back yard with a few flowers growing in it and a row of beans at the bottom. It was very dull.

Now it was a strange thing, but one of the gates of Fairyland was just beyond the bean-row at the back of Tom's garden. Fairyland begins and ends in all sorts of most unlikely places; nobody knows where. It is always just around the corner, and you see it when you are least expecting it. Certainly Tom never expected to see it anywhere, and wouldn't have believed it if he had!

Once you passed through the bean-row (the fifth plant on the right) you saw a bright golden gate, studded with shining stones. Through the holes of the gate you could see many pairs of bright eyes peeping – eyes of pixies and elves, wondering who you were and if it would be safe to let you in.

Now not far from Tom's bean-row, just

through the gates of Fairyland, there was a
land called UpandDown. You can guess what
sort of country it was – very hilly indeed.
Through it ran the Gnome Railway, a beautifully built track, with tunnels through the hills
here and there, and bridges across the rivers.
The little engines that pulled the carriages
along the track were very strong indeed, for
some of the hills were steep.

Many of the gnomes lived in caves in the
hill-side, and in order to get to the nearest
market town they used to take the train that
ran among the hills. So the little carriages were

always full, and UpandDown Land was busy and contented.

One day there was great excitement in the land. The King and Queen of Fairyland were going to come to UpandDown to visit the Prince High-Up, who lived in a great palace on the top of the highest mountain. That meant that UpandDown must be decorated, and everyone must put on their best clothes and wave flags. A special train was prepared to carry the King and Queen and their servants. It had two crossed flags in front of it, a gold funnel, and a beautiful carriage set with rubies that shone like lamps.

And then, the day before the King and Queen were due to arrive, a dreadful thing happened. Too-Tall the Giant came stalking along, and he chose to go right through UpandDown on his way home. His great feet squashed down everything they trod on – houses, shops, stations, it didn't matter what!

And one thing he spoilt was the railway! He trod on one tunnel and two bridges, and smashed them to bits, just as you would do if you trod on a matchbox! It was dreadful! It didn't take Too-Tall more than three minutes to walk through UpandDown – but you should

have heard the weeping and wailing after he had gone!

'What shall we do for the King and Queen tomorrow?' wept the little gnomes in despair. 'We shall never be able to mend those bridges in time and the tunnel will take weeks to repair. Their Majesties won't be able to visit the Prince. It is all very disappointing indeed.'

Only one gnome didn't weep and wail. This was Thinkabit, and he sat and frowned, puzzling to know what to do for the best, for he was the Chief of UpandDown and managed the little kingdom for Prince High-Up. Suddenly he got up and clapped his hands. Everyone became silent and listened. Thinkabit was going to speak.

'Friends,' said Thinkabit, 'this is a very sad thing to have happened just before the Royal visit – but I have an idea. Do any of you know the boy who lives in the house beyond the bean-row gates of Fairyland, just at the borders of UpandDown?'

'Yes, I know him very well!' cried Tickles, a small gnome in yellow. 'I've often peeped in at the window when he is playing by himself in the nursery. He makes the most wonderful things.'

'Yes, I have heard that,' said Thinkabit. 'Well, friends, what about asking this boy if he will come and build us two bridges and a tunnel before tomorrow? I have heard Tickles say that this child can build bridges, motorcars, engines, cranes – anything you can think of – in a few hours. He is just the one we want! Perhaps he would be willing to bring his tools and his shining bars and screws and plates, and build us our bridges and a tunnel?'

'Oooooh! Good idea!' cried everyone – but Tickles shook his head and looked doubtful.

'He doesn't believe in fairies,' he said.

'He might believe in them if he knew we

wanted him to build something for us,' said Thinkabit. 'Go and ask him, anyhow, Tickles.'

So off Tickles went, hurrying through UpandDown till he came to the great gates. He passed through them and pushed through the bean-row. It was night-time now, but the moon was full and shone very brightly. Tickles ran up the path and climbed up the ivy outside Tom's window. He tapped on the window.

Tom woke up with a jump and sat up. To his great astonishment he saw what seemed to be a small man standing on his window-sill in the moonlight. He got up and opened the window.

'Who are you?' he asked. 'Are you a dwarf from the circus?'

'No, I'm a gnome from UpandDown Land in Fairyland,' said Tickles. 'I've come to ask if you'll help us.'

'I don't believe in fairies,' said Tom. 'I think you are just a dream. Go away!'

'I'm not, I'm not!' said the gnome, in dismay. 'I'm real – as real as your meccano, Tom.'

'Are you?' said Tom doubtfully. 'Well, let me tell you this, little creature – I don't want to come and dance at any fairy ball, or sit on silly toadstools or anything like that. I wouldn't mind coming and doing something *real* – but – '

'Oh, it's something *real* we want you to do!' cried Tickles at once. 'You're so good at building bridges with your meccano – will you come and build us two tonight? Too-Tall the Giant has trodden on them, the careless thing, and smashed a tunnel, too. We want them all mended tonight, or new ones made, because the King and Queen are coming to Upand-Down tomorrow.'

Tom listened in astonishment. Then his face shone happily. Make some real bridges! Build a real tunnel for a real railway, although, of course, it would be very small. What fun! How perfectly lovely! Well, if fairies wanted things of *this* sort, he didn't mind believing in them at all!

'I'll come with you now,' said Tom, putting on his dressing-gown. 'I'll get the boxes of meccano. I know just which I want.'

He got them and then went with Tickles through the bean-row to UpandDown Land. When he saw the broken bridges he stood and thought for a moment. 'Clear all the mess away,' he ordered the gnomes. 'I shall build two completely new bridges with my meccano.'

He began. He fitted this together and that together and screwed here and screwed there. The moon shone down and the bridge glittered brightly as it slowly came into shape. It was the best one Tom had ever done. It went right over a deep little river, and was perfectly strong and steady, well able to bear the gnome train.

The gnomes were full of admiration and amazement. Tom went to the next bridge and looked at it. This crossed a narrow valley and was more difficult to do, as it had to be well fitted into two hillsides, and run for some way. But Tom was not at all frightened

of his task — no; he was a real engineer now and as happy as could be! The more difficulties there were, the more he enjoyed his job. It was splendid to work there in the moonlight, making real things for a real train, with all the little gnomes dancing around him, shouting in amazement at his clever work.

Then came the tunnel. This was very difficult, because Tom had to kneel down and try to see exactly what had happened. But he soon made up his mind that the best thing to do would be to clear away the broken pieces and the fallen soil and rocks, and build a strong inner lining in the hill, and then a tunnel under that, so that the weight of the hill would rest on the lining and not on the tunnel itself. Then it would surely be safe!

He had plenty of meccano pieces left. He found the most suitable ones for the tunnel and began to screw them together. The gnomes danced about, chattering in their little high voices. What a clever boy this was!

'There!' said Tom at last. 'I think everything is safely done. I say! It's nearly morning! The sun is just rising. I must hurry home or my mother will wonder where I have gone. When are the King and Queen coming?'

'Today at five o'clock,' said Thinkabit. 'Would you like to come and see them in the train, going safely over your bridges?'

'Oh, yes,' said Tom. 'It would be lovely to watch your train running over the bridges I have built and under the tunnel I have made. I will be here at five o'clock. Now I must go back.'

He took up his empty meccano boxes and went sleepily home through the bean-row. He fell fast asleep as soon as he got into bed, without even taking off his dressing-gown! His mother *was* surprised when she came to call him in the morning.

'Why have you got your dressing-gown on?' she asked him. 'Did you feel cold in the night?'

'No, I went to UpandDown Land and built some bridges,' said Tom sleepily.

His mother laughed. 'You've been dreaming,' she said. Tom sat up and wondered if it *had* been a dream. He dressed quickly and then went to look at his boxes of meccano. They were nearly empty. So it hadn't been a dream then! It was all real – and goodness gracious, he was going to UpandDown Land at five o'clock, after school that afternoon, to see the train there running over the bridges and through the tunnel he had made! How exciting!

Tom was very dreamy at school all that day, partly because he was sleepy and partly because he was thinking about the afternoon. At last, school came to an end and he ran home at half-past four. He had his tea and then slipped outside. He went down to the bean-row, pushed aside the fifth plant and found himself at the gates of Fairyland. They swung open for him and he went through. There he was in UpandDown Land again, and there were his bridges and his tunnel, shining brightly in the sunshine!

A whistle sounded, and a small train came into sight. The gnomes began to cheer like mad. Tom saw that the train had two crossed flags in front and a funnel made of gold. He held his breath as it came to the first bridge he had made. It ran steadily over it and the bridge did not even tremble, it was so well built. Then it ran over the second, longer bridge, and Tom cheered loudly when he saw that the train was perfectly safe on it. Then through the tunnel it went and came out on the other side.

The tunnel was quite near to where Tom was standing, and suddenly the train stopped nearby. 'Tom! Tom!' called a little voice. Tom knelt down and put his head close to the train. It was the Queen herself speaking to him.

'Thank you, Tom, for your work on our railway!' said the beautiful little Queen. 'May

we ask you next time we want any engineering done in Fairyland?'

'Oh, please do!' said Tom, blushing.

'Are you sure you believe in us now?' said the Queen, laughing.

'Oh, yes!' said Tom. 'It's all real here – as real as my bridges! I'll come and do any work for you that you like.'

And now, when Tom disappears and nobody can find him, you can guess where he is! He will be doing some building in Upand-Down Land, and if you want to find him, just push through the fifth bean-row on the right, and you'll be there!

The Wishing Glove

Peter was looking out of the window on Christmas Eve. He was feeling very sad.

'It's going to be a *horrid* Christmas!' he said. 'No holly, no pudding, no presents!'

'Try not to mind so much, Peter,' said his mother. 'Daddy can't help being out of work, and it's just as bad for all your little brothers and sisters as for you.'

'Yes, I know,' said Peter. 'I'm not bothering about myself, mother, truly I'm not – but I do so wish we could give Mollie and Peggie and Sandy and Jack a good time. Why, they haven't even got shoes to wear now! As for Daddy and you, I don't believe you've had enough to eat for weeks! And now it's Christmas!'

'Cheer up!' said his mother. 'Perhaps Santa Claus will remember us.'

Peter turned to the window again. He could see nothing but blackness – but suddenly he heard something. It was the sound of jingling bells. Nearer and nearer it came, nearer and nearer. Peter strained his eyes to see what sort of cart was coming by, but the night was too black.

'Jingle – jingle – jingle,' went the bells. 'Jingle – jingle and jingle!'

Then something passed like a flash and was gone. Only the bells could still be heard in the distance.

'Now what in the wide world could that have been?' wondered Peter. 'I'll just pop outside and see if I can find out.'

He ran out into the snowy road and looked up and down. Nothing could be seen, but he could still faintly hear the bells.

He turned to go back, when suddenly his foot knocked against something. He picked it up. It was large and heavy and soft, and Peter couldn't think *what* it could be.

'I'll take it indoors and see,' he decided. He ran into the house and looked at what he had found. It was an enormous furry glove!

'Good gracious!' said Peter, showing it to his mother. 'Look at this huge glove, mother! Whoever could have dropped it?'

'It *is* big,' said his mother. 'Whoever owns it will be very sorry he has lost it.' Then she laughed. 'Perhaps it was Santa Claus, Peter!'

'Santa Claus!' said Peter – then he stood still and stared at his mother.

'I believe you're right!' he cried. 'Those jingling bells must have been reindeer bells! Oh mother! Fancy finding Santa Claus' glove!'

He slipped the great thing on his right hand.

'Look, mother!' he said. 'Isn't it lovely!'

His mother smiled at him. Then she shivered, for she was very cold, and there was no fire.

'Oh, mother!' said Peter, despairingly. 'I

can't bear you to be cold. I do *wish* you had a nice warm shawl!'

Just as he spoke, a big red shawl appeared out of nowhere and draped itself warmly around his mother's shoulders!

Peter trembled with fright, and stared in amazement. His mother looked at the shawl open-mouthed. Neither of them spoke for a whole minute.

'Mother!' whispered Peter. 'Mother! You didn't have that shawl before, did you?'

'No,' whispered back his mother. 'Is it a trick you're playing, Peter?'

'No, no!' said Peter. 'I've never seen it before. It came suddenly out of the air, just as I was saying I wished you had a nice warm shawl.'

'Well, it certainly is a beauty,' said his mother, pulling it more closely around her. 'I haven't felt so cosy for weeks!'

Peter couldn't make it out. Then he suddenly caught sight of the big fur glove on his right hand.

'Mother!' he cried. 'I believe this glove's a magic one! I believe it's because I'm wearing it that my wish came true! Shall I try another wish?'

'Yes,' said his mother, eagerly.

'I do wish we had a nice warm fire!' said Peter.

Immediately the hearth was filled with crackling wood, and great flames roared up the chimney, sending a warm glow all over the little room.

Peter and his mother stared in delight. As they looked, in came all the children to see what the crackling noise was.

'A fire! A fire!' they cried with joy and ran forward to warm their hands. 'Where did it come from, mother?'

Their mother didn't answer. She was too

astonished and delighted. Peter laughed aloud with gladness.

'I wish for a fine big loaf of bread and a jug of boiling milk!' he cried.

Clap, bang! On the table appeared an enormous loaf and a jug of steaming milk.

'Ooh! Ooh! Look!' shrieked the children. 'Can we have some, mother?'

'Yes, yes!' she cried. 'Sit down in front of the fire and I will make you bread and milk.'

In two minutes everyone was eating bread and milk by the roaring fire. The children could hardly believe it, and as for Peter, he had never felt so excited and so proud in his life.

He told the others how he had found the

glove, and that he thought it must have been dropped by Santa Claus.

'That's why it's magic,' he cried. 'We can have anything we wish for!'

'Listen! Here's Daddy!' cried the children. 'Let's give him a surprise when he comes in, shall we? What shall we wish for?'

'Don't tell him about the magic glove!' said Peter. 'We'll just make him tremendously astonished!'

He thought for a moment. Then he wished.

'I wish that a joint of roast beef and roast potatoes were on the table,' he said. 'And I wish that a fine pair of warm slippers was by Daddy's chair!'

Immediately a joint of roast beef clapped itself on the table, surrounded by a crowd of delicious brown potatoes, all sitting in brown gravy. How glorious it smelt! All the children put their little noses in the air and sniffed hungrily.

By their father's chair appeared a pair of red fleecy slippers, ready to be popped on. The children pointed to them in glee, and were hushed by Peter, who heard his Daddy coming up the stairs.

The footsteps were slow and heavy, and sounded tired. The door opened and in came their father, sad because he had brought nothing for Christmas Day.

Directly he saw the big red glow at the fire he stopped in amazement. Then he smelt the roast beef, and turned his eyes to the table. He opened them wider than ever, and then rubbed them hard.

'Roast beef and potatoes!' he cried, wonderingly.

'And warm slippers, Daddy!' shouted all the children, pointing under the chair.

Their father walked to the table as if he were in a dream, and sat down. Peter pulled off his boots for him, and put on the lovely warm slippers, while his mother cut off a great helping of beef, and piled potatoes on a plate.

'Where did they all come from?' asked the astonished man.

'Never mind, never mind!' laughed Peter. 'Just eat your supper, and then perhaps we'll tell you.'

His father began to eat hungrily and soon his plate was empty. Once again it was filled, and he started on his second helping.

'Where did you get it from?' he asked.

'We'll tell you soon, Daddy, we'll tell you soon!' laughed the children, thoroughly enjoying the secret.

At last their father's hunger was satisfied and he drew his chair up to the fire.

'Now tell me,' he cried, holding out his hands to the warm flames.

'Well, first of all, look at this glove!' said Peter, holding out his right hand. His father looked at it in surprise.

'Now watch!' said Peter. 'I wish we had a big plate of cakes here.'

Immediately a large plate of cakes appeared out of nowhere and stood on their father's lap. He was so astonished that he nearly fell off his chair.

'Bless my soul!' he cried. 'Where did the thing come from?'

He caught hold of the dish and held it. On it were about twenty fine fat cakes that seemed to cry out to be eaten.

Everybody took one, and soon there was such a munching going on that nobody spoke a word for quite five minutes.

Peter finished first.

'I wish Daddy had a watch!' he cried – and before the surprised man could say anything, a brand new watch clapped itself into his pocket.

'I wish mother had a pair of fine shoes on her feet!' cried Peter.

At once his mother's old cracked shoes flew

off, and a beautiful new pair flew on. The children shouted in delight, and their parents smiled and stared.

'Stop! Stop!' cried their father at last. 'Tell me the secret of all this, Peter.'

Peter told him.

'I found the glove out in the road,' he said, 'and it's a magic one. I'm sure I heard Santa Claus go by, so I think he must have dropped it. I brought it in, and we've been using it ever since. That's the secret, Daddy!'

His father looked as if he couldn't believe such a thing – but he knew it must be so. He thought for a few minutes, and then he spoke rather gravely.

'There's just one thing I'm wondering about,' he cried. 'And that is – ought we to use someone else's glove like this? For all we know, we may be using up all its magic, and the person it belongs to may be very angry.'

'Oh! Daddy!' cried Peter, taking off the glove. 'I never thought of that. Do you suppose it really matters?'

'I don't know,' said his father, uncomfortably. 'I think we ought to try and find the owner at once, and tell him what we've done. That's the fairest thing we can do. We can give back the shawl, the slippers and the watch.'

'But we can't give back the bread and milk and cakes and meat!' said Peter. 'I'm rather glad we can't too – I did so enjoy them!'

'How can we find the owner, though?' asked his mother. 'Peter scarcely saw him, and it is only our guess that it is Santa Claus. We don't know where he is at all.'

The father laughed.

'That doesn't matter!' he said. 'We will just wish him here! Put on the glove and wish, Peter.'

The boy slipped on the big glove.

'I wish that the owner of this glove were here,' he said.

Immediately loud footsteps were heard on the stairs, and the door was flung open.

In came a fat, jolly-looking man, dressed in a red tunic.

'Santa Claus, Santa Claus!' shouted the children.

'Hallo, hallo!' said Santa Claus. 'Did somebody use my wishing glove, and wish me here?'

'Yes, I did,' said Peter, nervously. 'I found it in the road, and used it for lots of things. I wished for a fire because we were cold, and a shawl for my mother, and meat for my Daddy, and slippers and lots of things. Then Daddy thought you might be angry if we used up all the magic, so we wished for you to come!'

'Well, well!' said Santa Claus, taking his glove. 'I should have been annoyed, certainly, if you'd never told me – but as it is I'm most pleased that my old glove came in useful. I can't stop now, as Christmas Eve is my busiest night – but I shall come along again tonight when you're all in bed. So hang up your stockings, my dears, hang up your stockings!'

He laughed loudly, and ran down the stairs. Nobody spoke for a moment.

'Well, it was a good thing we owned up,' said Peter. 'I wonder if he really *will* come tonight!'

'Let's go to bed and hang up our stockings and see!' cried the children.

So they did, but although they tried their hardest to keep awake and see Santa Claus again, they didn't get a peep at him at all.

Still, they knew he had been, for you should have seen their stockings next morning! Nobody would have believed so many presents could have been crammed into such tiny stockings.

Even the cat had a present of a fine piece of red ribbon – so it's no wonder Peter's family believe in Santa Claus, is it?

Mr Woff and the Enchanter

Mr Woff lived in a big house right in the middle of the village of Trim. He was the head-man, and everyone admired him, for he was wise and good. His village was the best and the prettiest in the whole of the land. The gardens were full of flowers, the roads were well kept and the little shops were merry and neat.

Mr Woff was very proud of his village indeed. He talked about it wherever he went, and told everyone what a fine healthy place it was to live in, how all the flowers grew so well, and how nice the people were.

One day he went to a grand party at the King's palace, and found himself sitting next to a tall man in a pointed hat. This man looked rich, and he had piercing green eyes and a

very deep voice. Mr Woff didn't know who he was, but he began to talk about his precious village just as he always did.

The tall, green-eyed man listened hard and seemed most interested.

'Dear me!' he said, after a while. 'Your village of Trim sounds delightful. I've a good mind to come and live there. I'm selling my castle on Tiptop Hill and I'm looking for a nice quiet place to build another in.'

Mr Woff was pleased to hear this. It would be grand to have someone building a castle in the village of Trim! He would make friends with the owner and would soon be very grand himself. Oho! He rubbed his hands, delighted.

But he wasn't quite so delighted when he

heard who the green-eyed man was. No – his face fell and he looked quite frightened.

'That's the horrid enchanter, Too-Sly!' whispered a friend of Mr Woff's to him, at tea-time. 'Whatever do you want to tell him about our village for? It would be simply dreadful if he came to live there! Why, he would frighten the children, make horrid spells, bring his nasty imp-servants with him, and turn our nice, peaceful little village into a dreadful, noisy place! He's had to sell his castle on Tiptop Hill because people complained about him so. I'm sure *we* don't want him in our dear little village!'

Mr Woff stared at his friend in horror. What! Had he really been talking to the enchanter Too-Sly? Oh dear, why couldn't he stop talking about his village of Trim to everyone? Now Too-Sly would be sure to come and live there. He would build his castle there, and turn the whole village upside-down in no time!

'But perhaps he *won't* come after all,' said Mr Woff. 'Perhaps I shall get another chance to talk to him and then I'll say there's no room for anyone else in Trim Village.'

Poor Mr Woff didn't get another chance to speak to the enchanter, though he tried very

hard. He left the party feeling miserable, and
went back home, hoping and hoping that that
was the last he would hear of Too-Sly.

But it wasn't! The very next week there
came a short fat man to the village of Trim,
attended by two nasty little imps. He walked
all over the village and at last came to the hill
behind it. He had a good look at the hill and
then asked someone who owned it.

'Mr Woff owns all this village,' said the little
girl, half frightened at being spoken to by a
man with two imps behind him. 'He lives
down in the village, in that big house, there.'

The fat man went to Mr Woff's house and
knocked at the door, blim, blam! Mr Woff
opened the door.

'I've come to buy that hill behind this village, for my master, the great enchanter Too-
Sly,' said the little fat man. 'My master will
come tonight and stay with you, to pay you
for the hill. Will you please get all the papers
ready, so that we can start building his castle
tomorrow.'

Mr Woff didn't know *what* to say! He was
so upset, so startled to think that the castle
was to be begun the very next day. Whatever
could he do to stop it?

The little fat man gave Mr Woff a few

papers, bowed and went down the path. Mr Woff shut the door with a bang and sat down on a hall chair, pale and troubled.

How dreadful to think that because he boasted about his dear little village of Trim, Too-Sly was going to live there and make it a horrid place for the villagers! Whatever could he do?

His little wife, Twinkle, came up to him, surprised to find Mr Woff sitting all alone in the hall. When he told her what had happened she was in despair.

'We must stop him coming!' she said.

'But how?' groaned Mr Woff.

'We must frighten him!' said Twinkle.

'Frighten a great enchanter like Too-Sly?' said Mr Woff. 'Don't be silly. It can't be done!'

Twinkle went off to the kitchen to prepare a supper for the enchanter's coming. Mr Woff still sat on the hall chair, thinking. If only he *could* frighten Too-Sly! He knew that the enchanter would never live anywhere if he thought there was someone more powerful than he was, living in the same place. How could Mr Woff make the enchanter think he was even stronger than Too-Sly?

He thought and thought – and slowly a plan came to him. It was a strange plan, and Mr Woff wasn't sure that it would work. He thought he had better tell it to Twinkle, so off he went to the kitchen.

'I want to frighten the enchanter, as you said,' began Mr Woff. 'I want him to think I am a very strong and powerful man, so I've thought of a plan, Twinkle.'

'Oh, do tell me!' said Twinkle, mixing a cake quickly.

'Well – I'm going to put the cow in the cellar,' said Mr Woff. 'And I'm going to put the pig in the pantry. And I'm going to buy twenty tin trays and get my friend Jinks to come and drop them in the kitchen every five minutes!'

Twinkle stopped mixing the cake and stared at Mr Woff in alarm and surprise.

'Are you quite mad?' she cried. 'Whatever do you mean?'

'Wait, wait!' said Mr Woff, grinning all over his good-tempered face. 'Now, listen. When the pig grunts, as he is sure to do in the small pantry, I shall say that that is a wizard I have got prisoner, snoring in his sleep. When the cow bellows, as she will do, in that dark cellar, I shall say it is a dragon roaring down below, which I captured for a riding horse last week. And when Jinks keeps dropping the twenty trays in the kitchen, I shall say that is my giant servant, rattling his chains as he walks about the kitchen. Ho ho, that will make old Too-Sly shiver in his shoes!'

'Oh, Mr Woff, how clever you are!' cried his little wife. 'If Too-Sly thinks you've captured a dragon, taken a wizard prisoner, and keep a giant for servant, he will be very much afraid of you. And perhaps he will go away and never come back!'

Mr Woff went off to buy the trays, very pleased with himself indeed. He called in and told his friend Jinks what he wanted him to do that night. Jinks was delighted, for he was always ready to play a joke.

'You can climb up the kitchen steps every five minutes or so,' said Mr Woff. 'Then you can drop all the twenty trays from the top, down to the stone floor. My, they *will* make a noise!'

Then Mr Woff went to get his old cow, and to her great surprise he led her down to the dark cellar.

Then he filled his little pantry with straw, threw a few pieces of turnip and carrot into the straw and fetched his great pig. He locked it in the pantry and the fat beast stared round in surprise at his new sty! He couldn't understand it at all.

Mr Woff changed into his best suit, and then waited impatiently for Too-Sly to arrive. At half-past six a golden carriage rolled up to

his gate and out stepped Too-Sly the
enchanter, in a hat even taller and more
pointed than he had worn before, and in a
cloak that swept the ground as he walked. He
looked very grand, very powerful, and poor
little Mr Woff couldn't help wondering what
would happen to him if Too-Sly found out the
tricks he was going to play on him!

The supper was laid on the table. It was a
very good supper indeed. There were plenty
of pies, a great joint of roast ham, six different
puddings and ice-cream to finish up with.
Too-Sly was greedy and he was pleased to see
such a spread.

He and Mr Woff and Twinkle sat down to
the meal. Too-Sly soon began to talk about the
castle he meant to build. It was to spread all
over the hill, and Too-Sly said that he wanted
twenty servants from the village to help him.
Mr Woff knew that nobody would want to go,
and he listened in despair.

Suddenly there was a dreadful noise from
the cellar below the dining-room, where the
cow was. The poor animal couldn't understand what was happening, and, opening its
great mouth, it let out an enormous bellow of
rage.

Too-Sly dropped his knife and fork in a fright, and turned pale.

'Whatever's that?' he asked.

'Oh, don't worry about that little noise,' said Mr Woff, calmly. 'That's only my dragon.'

'Your *dragon*!' said Too-Sly, in amazement. 'What do you mean – your dragon? I never heard of anyone keeping a dragon before.'

'Haven't you?' said Mr Woff, raising his eyebrows in surprise. 'Well, you see, your excellency, I prefer to ride on a dragon, rather than on a horse, so I captured a fine dragon last week, and put him in my cellar. He makes a good steed, I can assure you!'

The cow bellowed again. The enchanter didn't like it at all. He went on with his dinner, and he kept looking in surprise at Mr Woff. Who would have thought that such a quiet little man would be able to capture a dragon and keep him for a horse? Too-Sly was most astonished. He jumped every time the cow bellowed.

'I hope your dragon is safely tied up,' he said at last.

'Oh, I think so,' said Mr Woff. 'Let me see – *did* I tie him up, my dear Twinkle?'

'Well, if you didn't, I did,' said Twinkle. 'I hope he doesn't escape, though, Mr Woff –

you know he ate two enchanters a month ago. It would be very awkward for his excellency, Too-Sly.'

Too-Sly really felt more nervous than ever. And when the pig in the nearby pantry began to root about in the straw and grunt for all he was worth, he choked with fright and went as white as a sheet.

Mr Woff banged him on the back. 'Don't worry about *that* little noise!' he said.

'But whatever is it?' asked Too-Sly, listening to the pig's loud grunts.

'I think it must be the wizard I've got prisoner,' said Mr Woff, listening. 'When he goes to sleep he snores terribly. Really, I shall have to make him stop sleeping.'

'What? Have you got a wizard here as a prisoner?' cried Too-Sly, putting down his spoon in amazement. 'What next! A dragon for a horse – and a wizard kept prisoner!'

'Well, your excellency,' said Mr Woff, helping himself to another piece of pie, 'the wizard annoyed me, you know. He *would* take the villagers for his servants, and they didn't like it. So I walked over to his house, put a spell on him, threw him over my back, brought him home here, and locked him up. I shall let him go if he promises to be good. If not, I shall give him to my dragon for dinner.'

Too-Sly stared at Mr Woff as if he couldn't believe his eyes! He felt very nervous indeed of this quiet little man. Good gracious! To think of Mr Woff throwing a wizard over his back and carrying him home! To think of him giving his dragon the wizard for dinner! Too-Sly's hands began to shake with fright. He wondered whatever Mr Woff would do to *him* if he didn't like him?

Then there came the most terrible noise from the kitchen, as Jinks dropped the twenty tin trays in a heap from the top of the kitchen steps. You should have heard it! It made even

Mr Woff jump, and he, of course, was expecting the noise.

Poor Too-Sly leapt right out of his chair and fell over, bump! He sat on the floor, very pale, looking at Mr Woff in alarm.

'W-w-w-w-what's that?' he whispered, looking towards the kitchen. Mr Woff pulled him up and patted him gently on the shoulder.

'Don't be frightened,' he said. 'That's only my servant giant. Whenever he moves, his chains rattle, and that was the noise you heard.'

'What! Have you a giant for a servant?' cried the enchanter, hardly able to believe his ears.

'Why not?' said Mr Woff, taking a large helping of ice-cream. 'A giant is strong and can do much more work than an ordinary servant. I have to keep him chained, of course, or he might get loose and harm the villagers.'

At that moment the cow bellowed again and the pig grunted loudly. Too-Sly began to wish he had never come to Mr Woff's house.

CRASH – BANG – CRASH! In the kitchen Jinks let fall all the tin trays again, and Too-Sly once again leapt out of his chair, his spoonful of ice-cream flying across the table.

'Pray don't be so nervous,' said Mr Woff, patting him. 'Surely you don't mind the rattle of my giant's chains! I will go and take them off him, if you like, and then you won't hear them rattling any more.'

Mr Woff got up and walked towards the kitchen door – but that was more than the enchanter could bear. He cried out in terror:

'Mr Woff! Mr Woff! No, no, do not take off your giant's chains! He might escape and do great harm.'

'Well – he certainly might eat you, Too-Sly, if he came in here and saw you,' said Mr Woff, stopping. 'I've just remembered that he hates enchanters, because one turned his mother into a frog. So perhaps he'd better keep his chains on.'

CRASH – BANG – CRASH! Once again Jinks dropped the twenty trays and once again the poor enchanter sprang out of his chair in a fearful fright.

'Perhaps you'd rather I didn't ask my servant to come and clear away the supper things?' asked Mr Woff. 'He might scare you.'

Too-Sly was in a dreadful fright to think of the giant coming into the room.

'P-p-p-p-please don't b-b-bother to have the meal cleared,' he stammered.

'Well, let's go into the study and talk about your castle,' said Mr Woff. He led the way and

Too-Sly followed, wondering fearfully if this dreadful man, Mr Woff, kept any strange creatures in his study! Too-Sly wished he had never, never thought of coming to live in the village of Trim. He didn't like to think of living near a man like Mr Woff, who thought nothing of catching dragons, capturing wizards or keeping giants for servants! He had quite changed his mind about wanting to build his castle on the hill nearby – but how could he get out of it now? He thought it would be very difficult indeed.

They sat down in the little study. There were many papers on the table and Mr Woff turned them over.

'Let me see,' he said. 'I think you wanted to buy my hill, didn't you? You want to build a castle there?'

'Well – I haven't *quite* made up my mind,' said the enchanter, staring at Mr Woff.

'But dear me!' cried Mr Woff, pretending to be quite indignant, 'you can't change your mind like this, your excellency! Why, I've all the papers ready! What has made you alter your mind?'

'I'm not quite sure that the air will suit me here,' said Too-Sly.

'But it's very good air!' said Mr Woff,

93

making up his mind to make the enchanter feel as uncomfortable as possible.

'Well – I'm really very sorry to have put you to so much trouble,' said Too-Sly, 'but I don't think I can live in your village after all.'

CRASH – CRASH – BANG – BANG! The trays dropped onto the kitchen floor again and the enchanter turned pale. He spoke to Mr Woff again, very hurriedly.

'But as you have gone to a lot of trouble for me today, I am quite willing to pay you one hundred gold pieces,' said he. 'That's if you'll let me off my promise to buy your hill.'

'Dear dear, this is a strange thing,' said Mr Woff, looking very sternly at Too-Sly, and enjoying himself very much indeed. 'Well, I am a reasonable man, and I agree. Pay me the hundred gold pieces, go out of my house and never come back again to my village of Trim. If you do, I will set free my dragon, I will tell the wizard to put a spell upon you, and I will send my giant to catch you! Perhaps it is just as well, Too-Sly, that, for your own sake, you are not coming to live here!'

The cow bellowed once more in the cellar, the pig grunted loudly and the trays crashed again on the stone floor of the kitchen. Too-Sly, very pale, thought it *was* just as well that he wasn't coming to live in Trim Village. He hastily counted out one hundred gold pieces on to the study table, said goodbye to Mr Woff, and ran out of the house to his carriage as quickly as he could, his cloak flying out behind him.

The carriage door banged. The horses started off at a gallop. In half a minute the carriage was out of sight. Then Mr Woff sat down in a chair and began to laugh. Twinkle came in and began to laugh too. Jinks came in with his trays and roared when Mr Woff told him the whole story. You couldn't even hear the cow bellow or the pig grunt for the laughing of the three in the study!

'Well, I've never told so many naughty stories in my life,' said Mr Woff, wiping the tears from his eyes. 'But if you're dealing with a wily and deceitful person, he can't complain if you borrow his habits for a short while! Look at all this gold, Jinks! We'll give a most enormous party tomorrow, and invite the whole of the village to it. That will be a fine way of spending the money! Ho ho ho!'

'Ho ho ho!' laughed the others, and it was a long time before they could stop.

And what about Too-Sly, the enchanter? Well, he galloped to the other end of the kingdom and didn't stop till he got there – and certainly he never, never again visited the pretty little village of Trim!

The Enchanted Forest

Roland and Gilly often used to stay with their Uncle Dru and their Auntie Rosalind. They loved going there because Auntie Rosalind lived in a cottage on the edge of a big forest,

and Uncle Dru could tell all sorts of strange, exciting stories of what went on there.

'There's odd folk in that forest,' he would say. 'My, there are brownies, goblins, gnomes and I don't know what besides, to say nothing of an odd witch or two. It's at the end of the world we live, and all sorts of forgotten folk peep out of that forest at times.'

'Oooh! I wish we could see them!' said Roland, but Uncle Dru shook his big head.

'Now don't you go seeking anything in the forest,' he said. 'There's plenty of adventures to be found there I've no doubt, but they're not the sort for you!'

'Gilly, come and help me with the baking,' called Auntie Rosalind.

'And you, Roland, come and help me with my digging,' said Uncle Dru.

'Oh, it's such a nice day, couldn't Gilly and I go off for the day and have a holiday?' asked Roland, looking longingly at the sunny lane outside the garden.

'Perhaps tomorrow,' said Uncle Dru. 'Today there is a lot to be done.'

That was the worst of Uncle Dru and Auntie Rosalind. They always found so many jobs for the two children. There seemed to be such a lot to do, and Gilly and Roland hardly ever had time to go off by themselves. Still, never mind, perhaps they could tomorrow. Gilly ran indoors to help with the baking, and Roland found a spade to help with the digging.

'You know,' said Uncle Dru, as they set to work, 'I used to have a most wonderful spade, Roland. My, it was a marvel, that spade was!'

'What could it do?' asked Roland, in surprise.

'Why, I had only to say "Dig, Spade, Dig, for your Life!" and it would set to work and dig all my garden by itself!' said Uncle Dru. 'It saved me such a lot of work!'

'What happened to it?' asked Roland, in excitement. 'Oh, I do wish I could see it!'

'Oh, a witch came by one night when I had left it out, and she took it,' said Uncle Dru, sadly. 'I've never seen it since!'

'I *must* tell Gilly that story,' said Roland. 'I'm sure she's never heard such a strange tale in her life!'

But Gilly had! She was listening to one that very minute. She had been helping her aunt to mix the butter and flour for the cakes, and had been stirring the dinner cooking in the pot.

'Once,' said Auntie Rosalind, suddenly, 'once, dear child, I had a most wonderful pot.

Oh, it was a marvel, that pot! You could put anything you liked into it – maybe just one potato, a bit of onion and a bone – and it would turn it into the finest meal you could think of! Fit for a king, with a smell that would make you so hungry you couldn't wait another minute for your dinner!'

'Oooh!' said Gilly, in surprise. 'I wish I could have seen it! Did it wear out?'

'No,' said her aunt. 'Pots like that never wear out. No, my dear, I washed it one evening and put it out on the sill to dry. A witch came by that same night and stole it. I've never seen it since.'

'I really must tell Roland that strange story,' said Gilly, excitedly. 'Fancy! A real magic pot that could cook a dinner out of almost nothing!'

When the children had each finished their work they ran to tell one another what they had heard about the magic spade and pot. How surprised they were to hear each other's story!

'I wish we could find the witch that stole those things,' said Roland. 'I'd love to take them away from her! Gilly! Shall we go into the forest tomorrow, and see if we can find where she lives?'

'I'd be frightened to,' said Gilly, going red with excitement. 'But oh, I'd love to!'

When the next day came, it was pouring with rain. What a disappointment!

'You certainly can't go out today,' said Auntie Rosalind. 'It's too wet. You must stay in.'

'It's a good chance for you to learn basket-making,' said Uncle Dru to Roland. 'I'll teach you.'

'And it's a good chance for you to learn knitting!' said Auntie Rosalind to Gilly. 'I'll teach you!'

'Oh, Auntie, oh Uncle, we don't want to learn anything today!' cried the children. 'Can't we read?'

'No,' said Uncle Dru, firmly. 'Basket-making might be very useful to you one day. You simply never know!'

'And knitting may be very *very* useful to you some day,' said Auntie Rosalind. 'You simply never know!'

That's what Uncle Dru and Auntie Rosalind always said when they wanted to teach something to Gilly and Roland. 'You simply never know when it will come in useful!'

'I'm sure I shall never want to make baskets,' said Roland.

'You don't know!' said Uncle Dru, taking some cane out of the water in which it had been soaking. 'I shouldn't be surprised if one day you aren't very glad indeed you learnt to make baskets.'

Uncle Dru's words came true, though Roland didn't think they would, as he sat rather sulkily learning how to weave the cane this way and that until he had made a fine little basket. Gilly sat patiently learning how to knit, and when the next day and the day after that both turned out to be wet, the children got on very well indeed with their new tasks.

Then there came a beautiful sunny day.

'You've been good, patient children, so you may go out this morning,' said Auntie Rosal-

ind. 'Be back for dinner. Here is an apple for you, Gilly, and one for you, Roland. Now be sure not to go into the forest!'

Off went the children – and oh dear, they disobeyed! Yes, they went into the forest by the very first path they saw! Wasn't it naughty of them?

They felt tremendously excited. They meant to find the witch who had stolen their Uncle's spade, and their Auntie's cooking-pot. They felt certain that it was the same witch who had stolen both things.

Presently they came to a curious house. It was built of round cobble-stones. There were some of red, some of yellow and some of blue. The chimney pot was black and looked for all the world like a big top-hat set on the roof. Gilly felt quite sure it *was*.

'Let's knock at the door and ask if anyone round about here has a magic spade and cooking-pot,' said Gilly. So they went up the little front path and knocked on the door.

A goblin woman came to the door. She had long, pointed ears, bright green eyes and a cross mouth. Round her head was a green scarf, and in her hand was a broom.

'What do you want?' she asked, crossly. 'I'm

in the middle of my dusting. This is a silly time to call!'

'I'm sorry,' said Roland. 'But I just wanted to ask if you knew of anyone in the forest who has a magic spade that will dig by itself and a magic cooking-pot that will cook a dinner out of nothing.'

'That's easy,' said the goblin woman. 'Why, everyone knows that Dame Tantrums has them! Where do you come from that you don't know that? If you want to borrow them, it's no good asking her, because she won't lend them. I've often tried to get them for a day myself, but the mean old thing won't let them out of her sight!'

Roland and Gilly felt excited at this news. So there really was a witch who had their Uncle's spade and their Auntie's cooking-pot!

'Could you tell me where Dame Tantrums lives?' asked Roland, politely.

'Follow the blue buttercups, and they will take you to her tower,' said the goblin woman. 'I should have thought you would have known that. Now, I can't stand here talking any longer, I've my dusting to do and seven children coming home from school in an hour. Good-day to you!'

She slammed the door and the two children

ran down the path. They had found out all they wanted to know!

'Where are the blue buttercups?' wondered Gilly, looking all round. 'Oh, look! There's one!'

She pointed to a strange buttercup not far off. It was bright blue. Another one was a little further on, and a third one further on still.

'This is the way!' said Gilly, dancing to the buttercups. Sure enough, it was! There were dozens and dozens of blue buttercups growing in a line through the trees and the children followed them for quite a mile.

Suddenly they came to a curious tower. It was built of pale blue stones, and had one little window right at the very top. There was a strange round door at the bottom, which was wide open.

'This must be where Dame Tantrums lives,' said Gilly. 'Let's knock!'

But nobody came in answer to their knock. 'Let's go in and see if we can find Uncle's spade and Auntie's cooking-pot!' said Roland. So they crept inside the tower, and looked around. But all they could see was a stone stairway winding round and round inside the tower. They went up it and up and up, and at the very top they found a door. It was open and they looked inside.

They saw a square room, with a bright fire burning at one side. There was a round table there, and a chair and two stools. A big bed stood in one corner, and a dresser with blue and yellow plates was in another.

Over the fire hung a black cooking-pot, and Gilly was quite sure it was her Aunt's! And in the corner by the dresser stood a big spade!

'That's Uncle's spade!' cried Roland, and ran to get it. But oh my goodness me! At that very moment, who should come in at the door but Dame Tantrums herself, the old witch! She stood and glared at the two children, then,

quick as lightning, she slammed the door and locked it!

'Ho!' she said, 'so you thought you'd come and get my spade and my cooking-pot, did you? Well, you've come, and now you'll stay!'

'No, please let us go,' begged Roland, feeling frightened. 'We wouldn't like to stay in this tower.'

'It doesn't matter whether you like it or not,' said the witch. 'I shall keep you here until I go to the Never-Never Land, and then I'll take you with me and sell you to the Never-Nevers!'

So the two children were kept prisoners in the tall tower. They were very miserable, especially as there were no books to read and no toys to play with. Gilly had to keep the room tidy, and Roland had to look after the fire, but that didn't take very long.

'I can't have you wasting your time like this,' said the witch. 'Can't you do something? Can you sew, girl?'

'Not very well,' said Gilly.

'Well, can you knit, then?'

'Yes, I can knit,' said Gilly. So the witch got out great balls of coloured wools and a pair of enormous golden needles. She gave them to Gilly and told her to knit a winter scarf.

'What can *you* do?' she asked Roland.

'I can dig,' said Roland.

'Ho!' said Dame Tantrums, 'well you won't dig in *my* garden! You'd escape, I know, if I let you down the stairs! Can you make baskets?'

'Yes,' said Roland, remembering his Uncle's lessons. The witch pulled out some cane from a cupboard and put it into a bowl of water to soak.

'You can make me a washing-basket,' she said. 'Now, listen – I am going away for three days, and when I come back I want to find that scarf done and that basket finished.'

She put on her tall witch's hat, wound her cloak round her and unlocked the door. She locked it again on the other side, and the children heard her going down the steps. They leaned out of the window and saw her flying away on a crooked broomstick.

They each started their work – and suddenly Gilly had an idea!

'I say, Roland! I believe that in three days, if I work very hard, I could make a scarf long enough to use as a rope to let down from the window to the ground!' said Gilly, excitedly.

'Ooh! What a good idea! And oh Gilly! I could make a basket to let down the cooking-pot and the spade in!' said Roland. So they

108

both set to work again with a will, and how excited they felt! If only they could get the knitted rope done before the witch came back, and if only they could let down the stolen things in Roland's basket, and take them back to their aunt and uncle!

All day long and far into the night the two children worked. At last they fell asleep over their work, and didn't wake up until the sun streamed in through the little window. Then they set to work again. Roland's basket was finished first, and he put into it the cooking-pot and spade. But the basket wasn't quite big enough so he added to it.

Gilly let down the knitted scarf from the window, and found that she had knitted just over half the length she needed. So she set to work again and knitted at top speed.

'Aunt and Uncle were right,' she said to Roland. 'You simply never know when anything is going to come in useful! What a good thing I learnt knitting the other day, and you learnt to make baskets!'

When the third day came the scarf reached nearly to the ground and Gilly knitted faster than ever to finish it before the witch came back that night. At last, just as the sun was setting, it was the right length!

'We shall have to be quick,' said Roland. 'The witch may be back at any minute now!'

They tied the top of the scarf to a big nail just inside the window, and then dropped the rest of it outside. It just reached the ground!

'You go down first,' said Roland to Gilly. 'Then I'll let down the basket with the cooking·pot and spade inside, and come down myself.'

So Gilly climbed outside the window, and swung herself on to the knitted scarf. Down she went, hand over hand, and at last reached the ground. Then Roland pulled up the scarf and tied his basket on to the end of it. He let it down and Gilly untied it when it reached

110

her. Then Roland climbed down the scarf himself, and there they were, side by side on the ground below!

'Good!' said Roland. 'Now quick! We must get away as fast as we can in case the witch comes back!'

They ran off quickly, Gilly carrying the cooking-pot and Roland carrying the spade. They followed the blue buttercups till they came to the house of the goblin woman. Then they knew their way home quite well.

Just as they got to the edge of the forest, who should they see flying in the air but Dame Tantrums herself! She saw them and gave a howl of rage. The children ran out of the forest towards their uncle's cottage as fast as they could. The witch knew that she could not catch them, and sailed off to her tower muttering angrily.

'Uncle Dru! Auntie Rosalind! We've come back home and brought your magic cooking-pot and magic spade!' cried Roland.

How worried their aunt and uncle had been, and how glad they were to see Roland and Gilly! They hugged and kissed them, and said they were wonderful children, and quite forgave them for being disobedient and going into the forest.

Roland and Gilly told them all their adventures, and when their uncle and aunt heard about the knitting and the basket-making, how astonished they were.

'Well, there!' they cried. 'What did we tell you? Didn't we say "You simply never know when anything will come in useful!" What would you have done if you couldn't knit or make a basket?'

They were so glad to get back their magic spade and cooking-pot. Uncle Dru went digging in his garden that very same evening with it, and Auntie Rosalind threw an old potato, a cabbage leaf and a mutton bone into the pot

– and hey presto! it made the most delicious stew they had ever tasted!

'Well, well,' said Uncle Dru, when they all sat down to it. 'You simply NEVER know!'

The Tale of Tinker the Pup

I am a puppy dog, and my name is Tinker. I am in disgrace, and I have been put in the corner; it is a great shame.

'Tinker,' my mistress said, 'you have been a very naughty little dog all day long! I am ashamed of you!'

Well, *I* don't think I have been at all naughty, and I am just going to tell you all I have done today, then you will know that my mistress is quite mistaken. I am a very good dog.

I woke up at six o'clock, and got out of my basket. I sleep with my master and mistress, and my basket is put in the corner of their bedroom. I felt a bit lonely so I jumped up on the bed.

The eiderdown tickled my nose, so I bit a

big hole in it, the nasty thing – and oh, do you know, it was full of the most exciting little feathers! They all came blowing out when I breathed on them. So I spent a lovely time chasing them, and biting them. I thought my mistress would be pleased when she woke up and saw how many I had caught.

But she wasn't! No, not a bit! She was very very cross! She smacked me hard, and said I had spoilt her eiderdown.

So I went downstairs to the cook. She was pleased to see me, and gave me a pat and a biscuit. I licked her hand, and then tried to fight her feet, but she wouldn't let me.

Soon I found a scrubbing-brush on the

floor, and didn't I have a game with it! I had torn all the bristles out before Cook found me.

'That was a fine brush you put down for me to play with,' I said to her. But would you believe it, she was very angry, and slapped me so hard that I yelped.

'You wicked little dog!' she said. 'Fancy ruining a lovely new brush like that!'

After breakfast I went upstairs to sniff round the bedrooms. I found a nice soft slipper under master's bed. So I pulled it out, and looked at it.

'Play with me!' I said. But it wouldn't. No matter how much I asked it to, it wouldn't play at all. I thought it was very horrid of it, and I gave it a bite just to show it what I thought. But still it wouldn't play.

Then I got really fierce and shook it hard between my teeth. 'I'll teach you not to play with me, you horrid, impolite thing!' I said.

I did teach it. It was all in bits before I had finished, and I'm sure it was very sorry it had been so horrid to me. Then – oh, dear! – the mistress came along.

'My lovely bedroom slipper!' she cried. 'Oh, you bad little puppy! You've nibbled it all to bits!'

I tried to tell my mistress that that was a good punishment for impolite slippers, but she wouldn't listen. She took me by the scruff of my neck and dragged me downstairs.

'I'll whip you the very next time you are naughty today!' she said, and she shut me into the kitchen.

Well, no sooner had I got there, than I smelt the *loveliest* smell I have ever smelt. It was SAUSAGES.

There was a long string of them on the table.

'I expect Cook has bought one for me,' I said to myself. 'Well, I'm hungry, so I'll have it now.'

I took the end one into my mouth – but they were all joined together, so the whole string fell down onto the floor.

'I'd better take my sausage into the yard in case Cook remembers about the scrubbing-brush,' I thought. So I tried to drag my one sausage into the back-yard – but all the other sausages came too. I couldn't make them stop coming.

'Well, if you *really* must come,' I said, 'I warn you, you may be eaten.'

I thought that would make them scurry

away – but it didn't. So I ate them all, every one. They did taste lovely!

But oh, Cook was crosser than ever I've seen her before. She took up a broom and gave me such a whack that I thought she had broken me in half. She hadn't though, and I scuttled out into the garden as fast as I could go.

'What horrid people live in my house!' I thought to myself. 'I've a good mind not to live here any more.'

Just then I heard a funny sort of noise, and in the next garden I saw a lot of fluffy yellow chicks. They were cheeping loudly, and making such a noise.

'Be quiet,' I growled. 'I have a headache, and I want to go to sleep.'

Well, those disobedient little chicks wouldn't take a bit of notice of me, so I squeezed my way through the hedge and went to tell them what I thought of them.

I ran at them, and they all scurried away, cheeping loudly. I thought this was rather a nice game, so I chased them all over the place. And then – my goodness – the fiercest old hen came up and was really very rude to me.

She flew at me, and pecked me on the nose three times. I couldn't seem to get away from her. But at last I did, and I squeezed through the hedge as quick as anything, with that horrid old hen pecking me all the time.

'It's no wonder your chicks are bad-mannered if they've got a mother like you!' I said. Then I ran up the garden as fast as I could.

I hadn't gone very far when I remembered that I had buried a bone somewhere yesterday. So I began to look for it. There was a lot of those red, blue, and yellow things about – flowers, my mistress calls them – and they were in my way. So I scraped a whole lot up, but still I couldn't find my bone.

Then I suddenly remembered where I had buried it, and I ran to the bed. Gardener had put dozens of little green plants in it – just like him to use my bone-bed for that – so I had to dig them all up.

It was just while I was doing that – and making a very good job of it too – that my master came out and saw me.

'You young rascal!' he said. Then he gave me three awful smacks, and carried me indoors to my mistress.

'He's dug up half the garden,' said Master. 'Put him in the corner, and tie him up for the rest of the day, my dear. He'll dig up the house next.'

So here I am in the corner, and nobody will
speak to me because I am in disgrace. But *I*
don't think I have been so very bad, do you?

Too-Wise the Wizard

Too-Wise was a powerful wizard. He knew almost everything, and he had travelled in every country under the sun and moon. He had met witches and fairies, enchanters and magicians, and never had he found any wiser than himself.

So he grew proud and boastful. He built himself a wonderful palace right in the middle of Fairyland, and there he made his spells and did his magic. Clouds of enchantments always hung over the topmost pinnacle, and little elves scuttled by quickly at night, for they were afraid of the wizard.

Not very far away was the palace of the King and Queen of Fairyland. They were angry to think that a wizard should come and live so near to them, but they could do nothing to prevent it.

One day Too-Wise decided to give a marvellous party, and invite to it all the witches, enchanters and magicians of the world. He had no right to do this, for they were not allowed in Fairyland unless Titania gave permission. But little he cared for that!

The invitations were sent out. This was one of them: –

TOO-WISE THE WONDERFUL WIZARD
invites
GREENEYES THE WITCH
to
A Party at his Palace. (Sports.)

'What sort of sports is he going to have?' everyone wondered. 'None of the witches or wizards are very good at running and jumping. It can't be that.'

It wasn't. The sports that Too-Wise was going to have were quite different. They were competitions in magic. He meant to show everyone how clever he was, and to win all the prizes himself.

The King and Queen of Fairyland were

worried about the party. They didn't like to think of all those witches and magicians in Fairyland. For, as you know, there are not very many good ones. So they put their heads together, and tried to think of a plan.

After they had thought for some time they decided that they couldn't stop the party. But they determined to send someone to it to watch all that happened, and report to them afterwards.

'We'll send Tippy the Elf,' they decided. 'He loves dressing up, and he is very sharp – he will notice everything.'

So they sent for Tippy the Elf, and told him what they wanted him to do. He was delighted, and clapped his hands gaily.

'What fun, what fun!' he cried. 'I'll make old Too-Wise think I am the greatest magician in the world!'

'But Tippy dear,' said the Queen, 'you know this is rather a dangerous task we are setting you. If you are discovered, you may be spirited away and never heard of again!'

'I'll take the risk,' said Tippy, but he stopped clapping his hands, and looked rather thoughtful.

The great day came, and with it arrived all the guests of Too-Wise the Wizard. You should have seen them! Most of the witches came on broomsticks, which were gaily decorated with ribbons in honour of the party. The enchanters chose all kinds of ways to come.

Some arrived on the backs of eagles, and some on rosy clouds. Some came in golden carriages drawn by goblin slaves, and some made the wind bring them. One came unseen by anyone, and suddenly appeared with a bang just by Too-Wise, as he was standing at the top of the wide stairs, receiving his guests. It upset the Wizard very much, and he gave the enchanter an angry glare.

'Not very polite,' he said, '*not* very polite!'

And what about Tippy the Elf? Well, he had

decided to pretend that he wasn't much of a magician, and to come on his feet, for he didn't want Too-Wise to notice him too closely in case he found out that he was not really one of the guests.

So Tippy, in big pointed hat and flowing cloak, humbly walked up to the front door, and took off his boots in the hall, for it was a rainy afternoon. Then he went up the stairs and shook hands with Too-Wise. The Wizard didn't take much notice of him, for just behind Tippy was a very famous witch, who had eyes in the back of her head as well as in the front, and Too-Wise was anxious to meet her.

Then there was tea. It was a wonderful meal. There was nothing on the table at all except empty plates, glasses and dishes, knives and forks and spoons. Too-Wise sat at the head, and asked for silence.

'You have only to wish for what you would like,' he said, 'and I have arranged that it shall appear.'

Then my goodness, you should have seen the things that appeared, when all the guests wished! A chocolate cake as big as a drum sat in the middle, and a red, white and yellow jelly appeared at one end, and a pink blancmange shaped like just a house at the other. It was wonderful!

Sandwiches shot up from nowhere, and strawberry ices jumped into the waiting dishes. One witch, who had a liking for pickled onions wished for a big jar of them, and they appeared just in front of her. But as it happened that the enchanter next to her hated the smell and sight of onions, they disappeared just as quickly – for he at once wished them away again!

The witch wished them back, and Tippy, who was just opposite, began to giggle when they disappeared again.

But he was hungry so he did a little wishing on his own account, and was delighted to see a ginger cake and a cream bun appear side by side on his plate.

After tea all the guests went into the great hall of the palace, where the competitions were to be held.

First of all there was a competition to see who was the cleverest at turning into something else. Tippy got quite frightened as he watched, especially when one witch near by changed very suddenly into a large cat, and scratched his leg.

'This is no place for me,' thought Tippy.

'My turn will come soon, and I shall never be able to turn into anything, for I don't know the right magic. I had better hide.'

So he slipped behind a curtain, and watched the party through a little hole he made with his penknife.

Dragons and unicorns, lions and tigers, beetles and bears, pranced about the hall, and then changed back again into witches and wizards. Too-Wise looked at them all scornfully, and then, muttering some magic words, he suddenly turned into a seven-headed giant. Tippy began to tremble. He didn't like it a bit.

'I've won *that* competition!' said Too-Wise,

changing back to himself again. 'Now let's get on with the next. Which of us has got the most wonderful thing in his possession?'

Tippy peered through his hole, and gaped to see all the marvellous things that were handed round. There was a needle that could sew by itself, a glass that could be filled with any liquid wished for, by tapping the rim, and a rabbit that could sing. There was a hat which made the wearer invisible, and a cloak that made him handsome to look upon.

But Too-Wise brought out a mirror, and set it before the guests. 'Think of what you will, and it will appear in the mirror,' he said.

Then in the mirror came a curious succession of strange pictures, the thoughts of all the guests around. Tippy wished the Fairy Queen could see it, for he thought she would love it. As he thought that, he saw her picture appear in the mirror, and everyone exclaimed in surprise.

'Who dares to think of that silly Queen at my party?' stormed Too-Wise. But everyone vowed that no thought of that kind had come into his or her mind, so the Wizard said no more. But he wondered very much, and cast a sharp eye on all his guests to see if any of

them were shams. It was well for Tippy then
that he was behind the curtain!

'I have won this competition too,' said Too-
Wise, boastfully. 'You will have to make me
your King! Now for the third competition. You
can each try and think of something I have
never seen! Ho ho! If you can do that, I shall
be surprised!'

Now all the guests were getting rather cross
with Too-Wise. They thought it was a shame
that he should win the prizes himself, and they
certainly didn't want him to be their king. So
they racked their brains to think of something
he hadn't seen.

'Hurry up, hurry up,' said Too-Wise.
'There's nothing you can think of that I've not
seen. You are stupid creatures compared to
me, Too-Wise the Wonderful Wizard!'

The witches and enchanters scowled at him.
They would have liked to turn him into an
earwig or something unpleasant like that, but
they feared his power. They were terribly
afraid, too, that he really *would* become their
king, for he certainly was clever.

They began to ask him questions.

'Have you ever seen the star-shaped lamp
that hangs in the deepest underground cave
of the dwarfs?' asked one witch.

'Yes, and I've blown it out!' said Too-Wise grinning.

'Have you ever seen the silver wand of the fairy who guards the Rainbow Path?' asked another witch. 'She keeps it locked up in a cupboard.'

'Yes, I have,' said Too-Wise. 'I stole her keys one day, and unlocked the cupboard to see the wonderful wand.'

'Have you seen the green wishing-carpet belonging to the Goblin King?' asked an enchanter, suddenly. 'It is said that none but he has ever cast eyes on it.'

'*I* have,' answered Too-Wise, puffing out his narrow chest. 'I gave him a spell he wanted, and in return he let me see his carpet.'

The witches and wizards sat silent for a moment. It seemed as if Too-Wise really *had* seen everything! Then a sharp-eyed one spoke.

'Have you seen the whistling fish belonging to the Prince of Dreamland?' he asked.

There was a pause, for none of the other enchanters had ever heard of this. But Too-Wise laughed.

'Ha ha!' he said. 'You're trying to catch me! The Prince has no such thing! I had dinner with him last week, and saw every one of his treasures – and there was no whistling fish!'

'You are right,' said the enchanter. 'I *was* trying to catch you, for you are too proud.'

'Have a care what you say!' said Too-Wise, frowning. 'If I become your king, I shall not forget those who treat me badly now.'

The game went on – but no one could find anything that Too-Wise had not seen. He sat there in front of them, vain and conceited, certain that he would become their king at the end of the party.

When the last witch and wizard had asked him their questions, there was a silence. Then Too-Wise stood up.

'I shall make myself your king,' he said. 'Not one of you is as wise as me.'

'We do not want a king,' said the guests. 'Least of all do we want you, oh, Too-Wise, Too-Vain, Too-Proud!'

'What!' cried the Wizard, in a rage. 'Well, think of something I have never seen, and I will disappear and never come back! But if you cannot, then I shall rule over you, and make you smart for these words!'

What would have happened next no one knows. But just as a witch was about to speak, someone near the curtain where Tippy was hiding, moved back a step, and trod on the elf's toe.

'Ow!' cried Tippy in pain.

In a trice the curtain was dragged back, and the elf, in all his fine disguise of pointed hat and cloak, stood before the surprised company. He trembled, for he knew that things would go badly with him, now that he was discovered.

'So ho!' cried the witch who had pulled the curtain back. 'Who is this?'

Tippy stepped out, and tried to look bold.

'I am a great wizard,' he said. 'Beware of me!'

Too-Wise laughed.

'Then perhaps *you* can think of something I have never seen!' he said, mockingly. 'Try to

think, or you will be turned into a droning fly. Quick!'

Tippy put his hands into his pockets, and wondered whatever he was to do. His right hand closed over a little red apple he had picked from his own apple tree that morning. And he suddenly thought of an idea.

'I will make all your guests laugh at you and your conceit,' said the elf boldly. 'Get ready to disappear for ever, oh Too-Wise!'

Everyone crowded around the elf, and Too-Wise scowled angrily.

'Speak,' he commanded Tippy.

The elf took the apple from his pocket, and placed it on the table.

'Have you ever seen the little brown pips in this apple of mine?' he asked, with a laugh.

Too-Wise stared at the apple in dismay. Such a simple question – but he could only answer 'No'! No one could see apple pips before the apple was cut. What was he to do? Everyone began laughing, and fingers were pointed mockingly at the wizard.

'It isn't fair,' said Too-Wise.

'Yes, it is,' said Tippy. 'You shouldn't have been so conceited, Too-Wise. Everyone heard you say that you would disappear for ever, if anybody could think of something you had never seen. Now, answer my question – Have you ever seen the pips in my little apple?'

'Answer, answer!' cried all the witches and wizards.

'I have never seen them,' answered Too-Wise, and as he uttered those words there came a rushing wind, and it bore him away for ever. How the witches and wizards cheered when he went! They were so glad not to have him for king.

They went home immediately, and Tippy was left alone in the palace. His first action was to take the magic mirror that had belonged to Too-Wise, and hoist it on to his back. He meant to give it to the Queen as a present. Then he ran quickly out of the door. He was just in time. As he went down the steps there came a strange whistling sound. Tippy turned to see what was happening.

The wizard's castle suddenly changed into blue smoke, and streamed up into the sky. It was gone!

'Hurrah!' shouted Tippy, and staggered off to Titania with his heavy mirror. 'What an adventure! Three cheers for my little red apple!'

Enid Blyton's
Enchanted Tales

THE MAGICAL SHOP

Three green goblins, Tuppeny, Feefo and
Jinks, set up a little shop which sells
anything in the world to witches, fairies,
elves and gnomes. Soon, business picks up
and the goblins' magical adventures
through Fairyland begin...

£2.99
ISBN 0 09 941095 8

Enid Blyton's Enchanted Tales

RETURN TO THE MAGICAL SHOP

News has travelled fast about Tuppeny,
Feefo and Jinks' shop that sells anything
in the world, and their orders are rolling
in. Their adventures introduce them to a
powerful enchanter, masses of magic and
to two very special pink pixie princesses.

£2.99
ISBN 0 09 941094 X

Enid Blyton's
Enchanted Tales

THE FARAWAY
TREE ADVENTURE

When Sly-one the gnome takes their
friend, Princess Fenella, prisoner, Peter
and Mary fly off to her rescue and on
an enchanting adventure through
the weird and wonderful worlds
of Fairyland...

£2.99
ISBN 0 09 940804 X

Enid Blyton's
Enchanted Tales

THE WIZARD WHO WASN'T

Bobadil the pixie wants to be a wizard, so in a nice star-patterned robe and tall black hat, he goes off to Twisty Town to impress the villagers. With no real magical power, but using his wits and pixie trickery, he becomes the town hero.

£2.99
ISBN 0 09 940805 8

Enid Blyton's
Enchanted Tales

MAGIC IN FAIRYLAND

Meet some clever townspeople, lots
of adventurous children, and a host
of goblins, imps, pixies and wizards in
this spellbinding collection of
tales from the magical
worlds of Fairyland.

£2.99
ISBN 0 09 940807 4